Table of Contents

The Perfect Score

The Perfect Score
By
Brett Shayler

The story, including all names, characters, and incidents in this production, is fictitious. The story intends no connection to actual persons (living or deceased), places, buildings, or products, and readers should not infer any.
Written by
Brett Shayler
Book Cover by Karen Shayler
To assist with the editing and design of the book cover, they used ProWritingAid, Grammarly, QuillBot, Canva, and Adobe Photoshop, all AI programs, to create this book.

Dedication

I dedicate this book to every young dreamer who enjoys showing dressage horses and dares to chase their passions, big or small, and to children who seek comfort and support in the steadfast friendship of an animal companion. This connection goes beyond language and nurtures a lifelong affection. This story celebrates those who possess the quiet determination necessary to overcome obstacles, persevere through setbacks, and believe in their potential, all while being supported by a loyal companion.

It is for the children who spend countless hours honing their skills, whether mastering a challenging equestrian feat, perfecting a musical piece, or building an intricate Lego castle—this dedication is for those who value initial commitment. During the mornings and late nights, hard work and determination help children achieve their goals, understanding that the journey is just as crucial, if not more important, than the ultimate success. It's a journey made easier and more rewarding with the unwavering support of friends, family, and animal companions, a reminder that dedication and support are key to success.

This book also celebrates the incredible bond between humans and horses—a relationship built on trust, respect, understanding, and a shared love for the beauty and power of the natural world. It acknowledges the patience, care, and consistent attention that went into developing this significant connection. This tale resonates with anyone who has felt the magic of a horse connection, shared peaceful moments, or enjoyed thrilling rides. May the following pages inspire you to reach for your dreams, nurture your friendships, and cherish the bonds that enrich your life. Diligence, commitment, and self-belief yield remarkable results.

This is the second book in my equestrian series, which follows performance horses and their riders. Each book explores the unique challenges and triumphs that young equestrians and their devoted companions experience. From the thrill of competition to the quiet moments of connection, these stories will celebrate the unbreakable bond between horse and rider, highlighting the lessons learned, and the friendships forged along the way. This book is for parents, guardians, and mentors who support and inspire young individuals' passion for showing horses. Your unwavering belief, patience, and dedication to their growth contribute significantly to their success. You can discover additional information about the trainers, the United States Dressage Federation, as well as any forthcoming shows. For your future dressage horse events, we have included the association's website, which is www.usdf.org, in order to provide you with help. We want to express our gratitude for your guidance, your unwavering support, and your ability to inspire them.

Chapter 1: Family Legacy and Pressure

The air hung thick with hay and polish, a familiar perfume that usually soothed Jammie. Today, however, it did little to quell the churning in her stomach. Her reflection in the polished brass of a trophy case—a case overflowing with her parents' accolades—mocked her. Each gleaming silver cup, each engraved plaque, whispered of expectations, a legacy she felt crushing her beneath its weight. This wasn't any competition; this was her first major solo Grand Prix in years, a daunting leap from the smaller, less pressured shows she'd competed in since she was a child.

Her parents, both legends in the dressage world, had been relentlessly supportive, their guidance often bordering on overwhelming. Their love was undeniable, a constant stream of encouragement with pointed reminders of their triumphs. "Remember your posture, Jammie, like your mother," her father would say, his voice a low rumble that vibrated with pride and a subtle undercurrent of demand. Or her mother's gentle but firm corrections, "More fluidity, darling, like your father. Elegance comes from within." Every comment, every well-meaning piece of advice, chipped away at her confidence.

She'd practiced relentlessly, pushing herself and her horse, Apollo, to their limits. Apollo, a magnificent dark bay with a temperament as steady as his powerful strides, was her rock, her confidant. He sensed her anxiety, his usually calm eyes reflecting her inner turmoil. Their bond was unbreakable, forged through countless hours of silence, a silent understanding that transcended words. But even Apollo couldn't completely erase the fear that gnawed at her.

The conversations with her parents in the weeks leading up to the competition were a constant source of anxiety. They spoke of her potential, of the opportunities that lay before her. Still, their words felt laden with unspoken pressure and a heavy expectation that she would match, if not surpass, their accomplishments.

"This is your time, Jammie," her father had said, his hand resting on her shoulder—a gesture meant to be reassuring but which only intensified the pressure she felt. "We believe in you. We know you can do this."

"Don't let the nerves get to you," her mother says, her voice softer, but her eyes held the same unwavering expectation. "Remember your training, breath, and the connection with Apollo."

But the fear remained. She'd secretly struggled with some performances lately, a nagging self-doubt creeping into her routine. Minor errors and hesitations that went unnoticed by others but played repeatedly in her mind, magnifying her imperfections. She compared herself to the photographs in the barn and the videos of their past triumphs, wanting to fall short of the ideal they represented.

The image of Karen, her rival, haunted her. Karen, with her effortless grace, her seemingly innate understanding of the movements, and her self-assuredness that radiated confidence like a beacon. Karen, who never seemed to doubt herself, never faltered under pressure—Karen, who seemed to glide through her routines with an almost ethereal beauty.

Jammie had seen Karen compete before. She possessed a natural talent that seemed effortless, a skill that appeared to come from within. Her riding was poetry in motion, each movement precise and perfectly executed. Her horse, a magnificent gray stallion named Zephyr, extended her will on how Karen held herself and controlled her horse with minimal effort felt like a stark contrast to Jammie's struggles and internal conflicts.

The thought of facing Karen added another layer of anxiety. It wasn't about winning; it was about proving herself. She needed to show that she wasn't riding under the weight of her family's name; she was creating her path, her own legacy, one graceful movement at a time. But the fear of falling short, of disappointing everyone, loomed large, a shadow threatening to consume her.

The pressure wasn't merely external; it was an internal battle, a war waged in the quiet corners of her mind. Each time she mounted Apollo, the weight of expectations settled upon her shoulders, heavier than any saddle. She'd see her parents' proud faces in the crowd, their eyes holding hope and a subtle hint of judgment, and she'd feel the urgency to live up to their dreams and legacy.

She sought solace in the rhythmic movements of her training, in the quiet understanding she shared with Apollo. However, the anxieties still seeped in, disrupting her rhythm and clouding her focus. Her usually precise movements faltered, the fluidity replaced by rigidity; the grace replaced by fear. She'd practice until her hands ached and her muscles screamed, yet the gnawing self-doubt persisted.

Sleep offered a brief respite. Echoing sounds of the Grand Prix arena, hushed whispers from the crowd, judging scores, her family's disappointed faces, and Karen's smug smile filled her dreams. She'd wake up in a cold sweat, her heart pounding against her ribs, the pressure of her family's legacy suffocating her.

As the day of the Grand Prix drew closer, the anxiety intensified. She retreated into herself, avoiding her friends, even John, her boyfriend, whose unwavering support usually calmed her fears. John understood her passion for dressage, her dedication, her struggles, and her self-doubt. He patiently listened to her anxieties, offering gentle reassurance and encouragement that felt like fragile lifelines in the swirling storm within her. However, his words had a limited impact. The pressure was almost unbearable.

Jammie knew she had the talent, the skill, and the dedication. She'd proven it countless times. But now, facing the glare of the spotlight, the anticipation of the judges, and the judging eyes of her family, her self-doubt threatened to consume her, overshadowing her years of training, her passion, and her connection with Apollo. This competition wasn't about winning; it was about overcoming her deepest fears, breaking free from the crushing weight of her family's legacy, and forging her identity, destiny, and path to greatness. And the battle had only begun.

Chapter 2: Meeting Karen the Rival

The stables hummed with a nervous energy, a symphony of clanging metal, hushed whispers, and the rhythmic thud of hooves on the well-worn earth floor. Jammie, clutching her riding crop, felt the familiar knot tighten in her stomach. She scanned the bustling scene, searching for a familiar face, a comforting presence amidst the chaos. Then she saw him—John, leaning against a stall, his calm smile a beacon in the sea of anxious faces. Relief washed over her.

John waved, his eyes crinkling at the corners. He pushed himself off the stall and moved towards her, his presence grounding in the swirling vortex of the Grand Prix preparations. "Hey," he says, his voice low and reassuring. "You look... tense."

Jammie managed a weak smile. "Just a little nervous," she admitted, trying to keep her voice steady. Reality proved considerably deeper. "It's this competition," she confessed, her voice barely a whisper. "The pressure... It's overwhelming."

John nodded, understanding flickering in his eyes. He knew her weight and legacy; she felt compelled to uphold them. He'd listened patiently as she'd recounted her conversations with her parents, the unspoken expectations, and the crushing burden of their past successes. "You're amazing, Jammie," he reminds her, his hand finding hers. "Remember that. You've got this." His words, though simple, were a lifeline, a small anchor in the storm of her anxieties.

Before Jammie could consume his reassurance, a sleek, gray stallion emerged from a nearby stall, its coat gleaming like polished silver under the barn lights. The horse was magnificent, its muscles rippling beneath its smooth hide, its movements fluid and graceful, even in its stillness. Behind it, a figure emerged—tall, slender, with an air of effortless confidence that sent a shiver down Jammie's spine. Karen.

Their eyes met, and Jammie felt a pang of something akin to fear. Karen's gaze held no warmth, no acknowledgment of their shared passion, only a cool assessment, an unspoken challenge. His gaze conveyed his dominance. The contrast between them was stark—Jammie, wrestling with self-doubt and the weight of expectations, and Karen, radiating an almost arrogant self-assurance.

Karen's presence was magnetic, drawing the attention of everyone nearby. She had dressed impeccably. She moved with feline grace, her every gesture precise and controlled, a sharp contrast to Jammie's nervous fidgeting. John, noticing Jammie's sudden tension, followed her gaze to Karen. "That's Karen," he whispers, his voice barely audible above the barn's cacophony. "Your chief rival. Heard she's almost unbeatable."

Jammie knew that. She'd seen Karen compete before, seen the effortless elegance of her riding, the seemingly instinctive understanding she possessed with Zephyr, her magnificent gray stallion. Karen's performances were poetry in motion, each movement fluid and precise, a seamless blend of horse and rider, a testament to years of training and an undeniable natural talent.

Karen, seemingly oblivious to their presence, continued her preparations, her movements precise and efficient. She adjusted Zephyr's tack with a practiced hand, her touch gentle yet firm. She spoke to the horse in indistinct murmurs, her voice barely a whisper, yet carrying authority and unwavering control. There was a palpable connection between them, a bond that seemed effortless and instinctive.

Jammie watched, her stomach tightening further. She had always admired Karen's skill, grace, and unwavering confidence. But now, face-to-face with Karen, Jammie's admiration turned to fear, a deep-seated anxiety threatening to overwhelm her. She felt insignificant, a shadow beside the dazzling star that was Karen.

Karen turned, her eyes meeting Jammie's. A fleeting smile played on her lips, but it wasn't a friendly smile, nor was it a smile of camaraderie or respect. It was a smile of superiority, a subtle assertion of dominance, a silent declaration of war.

"Apollo looks... well-meaning," Karen says, her voice smooth as silk yet laced with a condescending undertone. Jammie's breath hitched; it was a dig, a subtle yet effective jab at Apollo, implying he was not in the same league as Zephyr. Jammie felt her cheeks flush with anger, resentment, and a simmering mixture of emotions that fueled her determination.

"And Zephyr is magnificent," Jammie responded, her voice steady, although her heart hammered in her chest. Intimidation wouldn't affect her. She wouldn't let Karen's arrogance silence her voice and determination.

Sensing the rising tension, John stepped in. "Lovely horses, both of them," he says, attempting to diffuse the situation. He tried to inject a lightness into the air, but the tension hung heavy between Jammie and Karen, a silent battle of wills.

The conversation sputtered to an end, leaving behind a palpable sense of unease. Karen turned back to Zephyr, resuming her preparations with serene detachment. Jammie, however, felt the weight of their encounter pressing upon her, a tangible burden that added to the already overwhelming anxiety of the upcoming Grand Prix.

The contrast between them was undeniable—Karen's effortless grace, her seemingly innate talent, and her self-assured confidence were a stark contrast to Jammie's inner turmoil, vulnerability, and struggle with self-doubt. Jammie sensed their rivalry exceeded mere competition. It would test her will, resilience, and courage to face not Karen, but her inner demons. It would be a battle for self-discovery, a quest to redefine her legacy, one graceful movement at a time. In that moment, amidst the bustling stables, Jammie felt the competition's weight, the pressure of expectations, and her rival's looming presence, confirming her readiness to fight.

Chapter 3: John the Supportive Boyfriend

The air in "The Daily Grind" cafe hung thick with the aroma of freshly brewed coffee and the low hum of conversation. Usually vibrant and full of life, Jammie sat hunched over a steaming mug, her usually bright eyes clouded with worry. Across the small, round table, John watched her, his concern etched into his face. He recognized this anxiety differed from typical pre-competition nerves.

He had seen her at the stables earlier, and the contrast with Karen was striking. Karen radiated confident composure and effortless skill, while Jammie was tense. Even Apollo, usually so steady, seemed to pick up on her unease, his calm demeanor subtly unsettled.

"You okay, Jamie?" he asks softly, his voice a gentle counterpoint to the cafe's bustling atmosphere.

Jammie looked up, a flicker of her usual smile briefly illuminating her face before fading. "It's just... everything," she sighs, pushing a stray strand of hair behind her ear. "The pressure, Karen, the expectations... It's all piling up."

John reached across the table, his hand covering hers. Her hand was clammy and cold despite the warmth of the cafe. He squeezed gently, offering silent reassurance. "Your parents... they're putting a lot of pressure on you, aren't they?"

Jammie nodded, her gaze drifting to the swirling cream in her coffee. "They want me to win, to uphold the family name. It's like...a legacy I'm supposed to carry, and I'm terrified of failing them."

John understood. He'd heard the countless conversations she'd had with her parents, the subtle digs at her perceived weaknesses, and the constant comparisons to her older siblings, who had excelled in the dressage world. He knew how much it weighed on her, the unspoken expectations, the almost suffocating pressure to succeed.

"But this isn't about their legacy, Jamie." he says, his voice firm but gentle. "This is about your journey, your passion. It's your ride, your horse, your moment. Your success is yours alone to define."

Jammie looked up at him, a glimmer of hope flickering. He was right, of course. She'd gotten so caught up in trying to live up to their expectations that she'd almost forgotten the pure joy of riding, the thrill of competition, and the deep connection she shared with Apollo.

"I know," she whispers, her voice barely audible. "But it's hard to ignore. It's always there, a shadow hanging over me."

John leaned closer, his eyes meeting hers. "Then let's make sure your light shines brighter than any shadow," he says, his voice filled with unwavering support. "Concentrate on what's within your power. Your training, your preparation, your connection with Apollo. That's where your power lies."

For the next hour, he listened patiently as she spoke, offering only a safe space for her to express her worries. As she spoke, he learned of Karen's subtle jabs, the crushing pressure from her parents, and the all-consuming self-doubt she felt. He listened with empathy, providing understanding and support.

They talked about other things too. Their shared love for animals, their dreams for the future, and the simple pleasures of life. He spoke about his anxieties—the upcoming college application process and the pressure to choose a career path. He showed her that he, too, grappled with anxieties and expectations. In that shared vulnerability, a stronger bond formed, a connection built not on mutual affection but on shared understanding and unwavering support.

Jammie seemed to relax as the afternoon sunlight streamed through the cafe windows, casting long shadows across the floor. The tension in her shoulders eased, her breathing deepened, and the clouds of worry slowly lifted from her eyes.

"Thanks, John," she says, her voice soft but filled with a newfound strength. "You always know what to say."

"I listen," he replies, smiling warmly. "And sometimes, that's all someone needs."

Magically removing her anxieties, the pressure, and Karen's intimidating presence was beyond his ability. In his refuge, a safe space, she could shed her expectations and just be Jammie. He could remind her of her strength, talent, and passion. The significance of the action then dawned on him.

The next few days were a blur of intense preparation. Jammie spent hours in the stables, honing her skills and strengthening her connection with Apollo. She focused on her breathing techniques, posture, and movements, working towards a seamless harmony with her horse. John was there every step of the way, offering encouragement, ensuring she stayed hydrated, and providing a quiet presence of support.

Her anxiety betrayed itself through the subtle signs that he noticed. He possessed the remarkable ability to discern precisely when she required solitude and when she needed his silent, unwavering support. Despite his refusal to interfere directly in her training, he would always be present at the arena's edge, serving as a calming presence to ease her anxieties.

She would practice her routine, with John providing a play-by-play commentary that praised her strengths and offered constructive criticism for improvement in areas where she could refine her technique. He also helped her to prepare mentally. They discussed strategies for coping with pressure and managing nerves. He reminded her of her past successes, her unwavering dedication, and her incredible talent. Helped her reframe her thoughts to shift her focus from fear of failure to the joy of the ride, the beauty of the dance, and the thrill of competition. Helped her remember why she loved dressage in the first place—the freedom, the connection, and the sheer exhilaration of the performance.

The day of the Grand Prix arrived, fraught with excitement and trepidation. Jammie, dressed in her competition attire, felt a familiar knot of anxiety tighten in her stomach. But this time, it sharpened her focus and fueled her determination.

Because John was there, a sense of quiet confidence and reassurance filled the atmosphere, his presence a calming influence. As she and Apollo smoothly and gracefully entered the arena, he watched from the sidelines, captivated by their undeniable bond, the ease of their movements a testament to their connection. Her eyes showed him her firm resolve, intense concentration, and the quiet self-assurance that had grown from their many talks and private moments together. He felt a surge of pride watching her perform, a testament to his efforts. Watching her ride, he knew that no matter the outcome, Jammie had already won. She'd conquered her fears, faced her insecurities, and discovered the strength that lay within. She had found her legacy independent of others' expectations, a testament to her unwavering spirit. And that, he knew, was a victory worth celebrating.

Chapter 4: First Glimpse of the Grand Prix

A palpable nervous energy filled the air. Under the bright stadium lights, the Grand Prix arena's meticulously groomed sand shimmered across its vast expanse. A tiered amphitheater of faces, the stands, hummed with anticipation, a sea of quiet whispers and hushed exclamations. Amidst the throng, Jammie felt a surge of excitement and apprehension. Years of training led to this, the final trial of skill and nerve. Right now, she's a passive observer of expert work.

A seasoned professional named Jammie, whose name appeared on many magazine covers and online videos, was the first rider to enter the arena. The horse, a magnificent black stallion, moved with an effortless grace that seemed to defy gravity. Their movements were fluid and seamless, a breathtaking ballet of power and precision.

Jammie watched, mesmerized, her anxieties momentarily forgotten in the sheer artistry of the performance. The crowd erupted in applause as the rider completed their routine, a thunderous ovation that shook the stadium's foundations.

She spent the next few hours completely absorbed in the spectacle. Each rider brought a unique style and a distinct personality to their performance. Some were powerful and dramatic, their horses thundering across the arena in a display of raw strength and athleticism. Riders performed refined routines, their movements precise and controlled, each step a testament to years of meticulous training. The diversity of styles and approaches captivated Jammie, showcasing the depth and complexity of dressage as a sport.

She noticed subtle details she'd never fully appreciated before—the almost imperceptible shifts in the rider's weight, the delicate adjustments of the reins, and the unwavering focus in their eyes. It was a dance of subtle nuances, a conversation between horse and rider, a silent dialogue expressed through precise and controlled movements that seemed almost magical. In these details, the careful choreography of the performance revealed the true artistry of dressage.

The intensity of the competition was palpable. The air thrummed with the riders' energy, the spectators' nervous tension, and the hushed whispers of anticipation. Jammie could feel the pressure radiating from the arena, the weight of expectations bearing down on each competitor. She watched some riders perform flawlessly, their routines a symphony of controlled power and effortless grace. Others struggled, their horses resisting, their movements faltering under the weight of the pressure. The stark contrasts of success and failure offered a poignant lesson in resilience and determination.

During a break in the competition, Jammie stood next to another young rider. She was slightly older, maybe eighteen or nineteen, with a quiet confidence that belied her youth. They introduced themselves; the girl's name was Sarah. Sarah was also competing in the upcoming regional championships, a class different from Jammie's, but they shared a bond over their love of the sport.

Sarah discussed the pressures of competition, the relentless training, and the constant pursuit of perfection. She spoke of the intense scrutiny, the judging, and the inevitable disappointment that comes with not meeting expectations. It was reassuring to hear someone else's voice express the same anxieties, to know she wasn't alone in her feelings. Sarah, however, conveyed a calm maturity Jammie envied. Trophies didn't define her passion for dressage, but her deep connection with her horse did. She spoke of the quiet moments in the stables, the shared glances, the unspoken understanding between them.

Jammie shared some of her anxieties—the pressure from her parents, her fear of letting them down, her fierce competition with Karen. Sarah listened patiently, her eyes reflecting both empathy and understanding. She shared her struggles with self-doubt and moments of crippling fear, reminding Jammie that such emotions were a natural part of the process. Instead of minimizing the struggles, Sarah acknowledged them, offering a perspective that shifted Jammie's viewpoint. It wasn't about avoiding anxiety, but about learning to manage it, to use it as fuel to drive her forward rather than let it paralyze her.

Their conversation extended far beyond the mere competition, leading to a discussion of their life beyond the arenas, their studies, and their friendships.

The shared passion for horses and their common anxieties bridged a gap, forging an unexpected connection between the girls. As the conversation wound down, Jammie felt a sense of relief. The Grand Prix, still unfolding around them, was no longer a spectacle of pressure and judgment, but a shared experience, a testament to the power of human connection.

Another rider, a tall, slender young man with a kind smile, joined their conversation. He introduced himself as Liam. Liam's approach to the sport seemed more laid-back, yet incredibly effective. He spoke of his connection with his horse as a partnership rather than competition, focusing on the joy and harmony in their shared performance. He shared anecdotes of his training sessions, emphasizing the importance of patience, understanding, and mutual respect. His enthusiasm was infectious, subtly lightening the atmosphere of quiet apprehension Jammie had been feeling.

Their conversations helped Jammie shift her perspective on the competition. It was no longer merely a contest of skill, but a celebration of dedication, resilience, and the powerful bond between horse and rider. The intensity and pressure remained, but the shared experience of the other young riders, especially Sarah and Liam, grounded her anxieties, transforming fear into quiet determination. This shift in perspective would prove crucial in the days to come.

Both captivating and emotionally charged, the Grand Prix concluded with unforgettable final performances. The riders poured their hearts and souls into their routines, their dedication visible in every carefully executed movement. The crowd responded with thunderous applause, their cheers a testament to the skill and passion displayed on the arena floor.

While observing, Jammie sensed the crowd's energy and excitement filling the expansive space. It was a palpable emotion that was as significant as the actual performance.

Jammie felt exhausted, yet exhilarated, when the final rider exited. The Grand Prix had been a powerful reminder of the dedication, skill, and resilience required to compete at the highest levels of dressage. Despite the challenges and anxieties, it was an affirmation of her chosen path. She left the arena with a renewed sense of purpose, a deeper understanding of herself and her relationship with Apollo, and a quiet confidence that whispered of what lay ahead. The upcoming competition wouldn't be easy, but she was ready.

Chapter 5: Preparing for the Competition

The following days blurred into a whirlwind of intense preparation. The Grand Prix loomed, a colossal shadow stretching over every waking moment. My meticulously planned schedule was a relentless cycle: early morning rises for sunrise rides with Apollo, followed by hours of intense training under the watchful eye of Coach Miller. The air hung heavy with anticipation, the quiet hum of the stables a stark contrast to the storm brewing within me.

Apollo, my magnificent chestnut gelding, was as much a part of this preparation as I was. He sensed the shift in my energy, the heightened urgency in my movements. A focused intensity tempered his usually playful spirit, mirroring my own. Our training sessions were less about perfecting individual movements and more about forging a seamless unity, a symbiotic connection that transcended the physical.

Coach Miller, a woman whose unwavering gaze could penetrate even the most carefully constructed façade, pushed me harder than ever. She didn't correct my posture and refine my technique; she worked on my mental fortitude, honing the subtle nuances of control and confidence. "Dressage is as much a mental game as a physical one, Jammie," she'd say, her voice a low rumble that resonated with quiet authority. "You can have the most perfect horse, the most flawless technique, but if your mind falters, your performance will crumble."

Her words resonated deeply. Pressure mounted, a relentless weight pressing down on my shoulders. The weight of expectation, the whispers of doubt, the fear of failure—all coalesced into a suffocating cloud. I battled not the physical demands of the training, but the internal demons that threatened to unravel me.

The days bled into each other, a relentless cycle of training, stretching, physiotherapy, and endless repetitions of the Grand Prix movements. My body ached, my muscles screamed in protest, but I pushed forward, fueled by a desperate need to prove myself and overcome the nagging self-doubt that haunted my every step. My muscle memory keeps the meticulously crafted choreography of the Grand Prix. I wasn't riding; I was becoming one with Apollo, a seamless fusion of horse and rider, a partnership forged in sweat, determination, and shared ambition.

Each evening, I spent time meticulously reviewing videos of past performances and critically analyzing my strengths and weaknesses. I dissected every movement, every nuance, searching for those elusive areas that needed improvement. The rhythmic clicking of the mouse and the hushed concentration of my post-training review sessions became a ritual, a testament to the single-minded focus that consumed me.

John, my boyfriend, was my anchor in this storm of preparation. He understood the sacrifices I was making, the immense pressure I was under. He didn't diminish my anxieties or sugarcoat the challenges; instead, he provided unwavering support, a quiet presence that calmed my nerves and replenished my spirit. His brief stable visits offered respite from rigorous training. We would walk Apollo together, discussing our respective activities, and John's calm presence grounded me. He would meticulously braid Apollo's mane, his gentle touch a soothing contrast to the rigorous nature of my training regime. His patience and understanding were vital in my preparations, as they balanced my drive with my need for human connection and affection.

The bond with Apollo deepened during this period. We spent hours in the stables, not riding but simply being together. We would groom him together, carefully brushing away the sweat and dirt, whispering reassurances, connecting on a deeper level beyond the usual trainer-horse relationship. His soft, warm breath against my cheek and the comforting weight of his head resting on my shoulder—these small moments were a vital source of strength. These seemingly mundane actions were more significant than any medal or trophy could be. This connection became my foundation, the unbreakable support that reassured me of our shared journey.

Karen, my ever-present rival, remained a constant reminder of the stakes. I would catch glimpses of her during my training sessions, her presence a silent challenge that fueled my competitive spirit. Her confidence was undeniable, her skill impeccable, but her arrogance was a glaring flaw. I focused on my performance, striving for perfection not to surpass her, but to surpass my limitations.

As the competition drew nearer, the atmosphere at the stables became charged with excitement and apprehension. Riders sharpened their skills. People meticulously groomed the horses, and a palpable anticipation crackled in the air. Every day brought a new level of stress, testing my endurance and resilience. My sleep was restless, plagued by vivid dreams of botched performances and catastrophic falls. My anxiety often caused me to jump awake, my body tense, but I reassured myself each time that I was prepared. Apollo, too, seemed more tense, but his responses to my commands were impeccable. The unspoken understanding between us was stronger than ever.

Coach Miller noticed my growing anxiety. To boost confidence, she added sessions on mental conditioning, pressure management, and visualization. Breathing exercises, guided by her, helped me center myself and reduce my rapid heartbeat. She helped me remember the Grand Prix wasn't about skill, but the culmination of years of training, dedication, and my unshakeable bond with Apollo.

The final days were a blur of last-minute checks, equipment adjustments, and a relentless review of my routine. I ingrained each movement and transition in my muscles; they echoed in the quiet spaces between my breaths. The weight of expectations remained, but a growing sense of readiness, a calm confidence that whispered through the anxiety, tempered it, urging me forward.

My ride wasn't personal; it represented our collaboration with Apollo, John, Coach Miller's steadfast backing, plus our upcoming shared endeavor. The Grand Prix was not a competition; it was a testament to the dedication, resilience, and unbreakable bond between a girl and her horse.

Chapter 6: Internal Struggles and Self-Doubt

The polished gleam of Apollo's coat reflected the harsh fluorescent lights of the indoor arena, a stark contrast to the turmoil raging within me. Each perfectly executed piaffe, each effortless passage, felt hollow, a mere imitation of the grace and fluidity I yearned for. My movements, which were usually fluid and precise, had now become jerky and hesitant, betraying the tremor in my hands. Coach Miller's encouraging words, usually a source of strength, now felt like hollow platitudes, bouncing off the walls of my self-doubt.

The pressure was crushing. Not the pressure to perform flawlessly in front of the judges, the spectators, and Karen, whose smug smile seemed to follow me like a shadow, but the pressure to live up to the legacy of my family, a legacy built on generations of equestrian excellence. My mind magnified every mistake, every minor imperfection, transforming a simple stumble into a catastrophic failure.

My internal monologue became a relentless chorus of self-criticism.

You're not good enough. You'll mess up. Everyone will see how inadequate you are. These insidious whispers, amplified by the mounting pressure, gnawed at my confidence, eroding my belief in my ability to succeed. I felt like a tightrope walker, precariously balanced on a thin line, with the abyss of failure yawning beneath me. Each training session was a torturous exercise in self-doubt, a battle between my will to succeed and the insidious voice that whispered of inevitable defeat.

Even Apollo sensed the shift in my demeanor. His usually responsive movements were hesitant, his energy subdued. He mirrored my anxiety, his typically bright eyes clouded with a tentative uncertainty. He seemed to understand my internal battle, a silent, empathetic partner in my struggle. Our usually effortless connection felt strained, fragmented by my self-imposed barriers. The fluid grace of our past performances felt like a distant memory, replaced by a stiff, almost robotic rigidity.

I retreated further into myself, avoiding the other riders; their easy banter and playful competition felt like a painful reminder of my inadequacy. Karen's unwavering confidence seemed to taunt me, a constant, unwelcome presence that amplified my insecurity. Her effortless grace in the saddle and sharp precision were a continual reminder of the gulf that separated our performances, not merely a difference in skill, but also confidence and self-belief.

Nights were worse. Sleep evaded me, replaced by a restless anxiety that kept me from tossing and turning. My dreams were a kaleidoscope of missed cues, botched routines, and catastrophic falls, each nightmare leaving me drenched in sweat and trembling with a lingering dread. I would wake up with a start, heart pounding, the echoes of my internal monologue still ringing in my ears. The rising sun, a symbol of hope for others, felt like a cruel reminder of the approaching competition, the impending test of my self-worth.

During the day, the pressure to mask my anxieties added another layer to the struggle. I put on a brave face, plastering a smile over my fear, but a thin facade crumbled under the weight of my internal turmoil. I tried to project an image of calm confidence, but my carefully constructed poise felt fragile, threatening to shatter at any moment. The other riders, oblivious to my internal turmoil, seemed to float through their training sessions with effortless ease, their relaxed confidence starkly contrasting my simmering anxiety.

Even John's unwavering support felt inadequate. He listened patiently as I poured out my fears and frustrations, offering encouragement, reminding me of my past successes, and reiterating his belief in my capabilities. But his words, while well-intentioned, felt like weak reassurances, powerless to quell the storm raging within me. I felt guilty for burdening him with my anxieties, for dampening his enthusiasm with my self-doubt. The guilt only intensified the pressure, reinforcing the negative thoughts that tormented me.

Desperate for a solution, I sought Coach Miller, confessing my fears, my anxieties, and my crippling self-doubt. She listened patiently, her gaze unwavering, her understanding surpassing my expectations. She didn't dismiss my worries or minimize my anxieties. She reminded me that self-doubt was a common experience, especially among highly driven individuals, and that acknowledging and addressing those feelings was crucial to overcoming them.

Coach Miller introduced me to visualization techniques, urging me to create mental images of successful performances, visualizing each movement and transition with unwavering precision. To help me manage my anxiety, she recommended meditation and deep breathing, suggesting ways to ground myself and quiet my inner turmoil. These exercises weren't for removing fear, but for learning to control it, changing it from a debilitating obstacle to a surmountable difficulty.

She emphasized the importance of staying in the present, letting go of past mistakes and future worries to focus only on each movement, each task, each breath. She reminded me that dressage was as much a mental game as a physical one, and that my mindset would ultimately shape my performance. It was not just about technique and skill, but also about mastering my mental game. The focus shifted from perfection to process, from outcome to present moment, empowering me to relinquish my relentless self-criticism.

The days that followed were less about physical training and more about mental preparation. I spent hours practicing visualization techniques, creating vivid mental images of successful performances, feeling the strength of Apollo's body beneath me, and sensing the rhythm of our movements. I practiced deep breathing exercises, learning to control my racing pulse and calm my agitated mind. Slowly but surely, calm settled over me, a quiet confidence replacing the paralyzing fear. The intense, consuming self-doubt receded, giving way to a growing sense of readiness. The fear hadn't completely disappeared; it was simply more manageable. I was learning to coexist with and harness it rather than let it consume me.

As the Grand Prix drew closer, I approached each training session not with dread and self-doubt, but with a newfound acceptance and a quiet determination. The challenge remained daunting but manageable, an obstacle to overcome rather than an insurmountable barrier. I still struggled with the insidious whispers of self-doubt returning, but I had learned to recognize and address them, to redirect my thoughts, to regain my focus. The Grand Prix wasn't about winning; it was about conquering my self-doubt and proving to myself that I could overcome my fear, harnessing the immense power within. My journey had transformed from one of self-doubt to one of self-discovery.

The path ahead was more straightforward, paved with the growing realization that I was capable, resilient, and ready to face whatever lay ahead. My preparation was complete, or as complete as it would ever be. I was ready.

Chapter 7: Karen's Taunts and Intimidation

The air in the stables hung thick with the scent of hay, sweat, and anticipation. The rhythmic clip-clop of hooves on the wooden floors provided a counterpoint to the nervous energy that thrummed beneath the surface. Everywhere I looked, riders were meticulously preparing their horses — a flurry of activity that usually excited me, now serving only to amplify my unease. Karen, of course, was the exception. She moved with an unnerving grace, a feline sleekness that seemed to mock my clumsy efforts.

Her presence felt like constant, subtle pressure, a weight bearing down on me, even when she wasn't directly interacting with me. She meticulously groomed her horse, a magnificent black stallion named Midnight. Her movements were precise and deliberate, each exuding an air of effortless superiority. Her sharp and brittle laughter carried efficiently across the stables, a jarring dissonance to my quiet anxieties.

"Looking a little pale, Jammie," she'd say, her voice dripping with feigned concern, her eyes gleaming with amusement. "Nervous about the Grand Prix? I wouldn't be. It's practically a guaranteed win for me." She'd pause, letting her words hang in the air. A subtle jab aimed at my confidence.

Her actions went beyond verbal barbs. She'd subtly sabotage my preparations, bumping into me as I carried buckets of water, "accidentally" brushing against Apollo's sensitive flanks as I worked with him. These actions were subtle, easily dismissed as clumsy accidents, yet they unsettled me, each incident adding another layer of tension to my already frayed nerves. Once, she even "accidentally" spilled a bucket of water near my tack, the soggy leather a constant reminder of her subtle acts of aggression. I couldn't prove anything, and voicing my suspicions would only make me appear paranoid and weak.

It wasn't her actions themselves. Just her presence heightened my anxiety. The way she executed each complex movement with ease, her horse responding to the slightest cue with flawless precision, felt like a sharp reminder of my own shortcomings. Her unwavering self-assurance was a constant reminder of the gap between her skill and my self-doubt. I felt like I was constantly being evaluated and judged. Each perfectly executed movement was a silent condemnation of my struggle for perfection.

Her annoyance stemmed from even insignificant matters. One morning, I accidentally left my water bottle near her stall. She didn't merely move it; she flung it across the stable, the water splashing onto the hay bales. Her eyes met mine for a split second, a flicker of malice in their depths before she turned away, resuming her grooming as though nothing had happened.

The other riders seemed oblivious, primarily to Karen's subtle (and not-so-subtle) intimidation tactics, or perhaps they ignored them. Some even seemed to admire her confidence and view her arrogance as a sign of her unwavering self-belief. Their silence added to the isolation; their indifference was a tacit approval of Karen's behavior.

The pressure was immense, a vise squeezing the air from my lungs.

I felt like I was drowning in a sea of self-doubt, her constant presence a relentless undertow pulling me down. I tried to focus on my training, on Apollo and the upcoming competition, but Karen's shadow loomed over every movement, every breath.

Evenings were the worst. Sleep offered a little rest. The exhaustion compounded the anxiety; the exhaustion adding to my physical and emotional strain.

Throughout the storm, John, my ever-loyal boyfriend, was my constant support. Patiently, he heard my trembling, angry, and fearful frustrations. Offering comfort and reassurance, he reminded me of my skills, past wins, and what I could achieve. The gentle massage he gave my shoulders eased the tension, his touch a blessing and a physically showing off his emotional support.

"She's jealous," he'd say, his voice a calm counterpoint to the tempest within me. "You're talented, Jammie. You're amazing. Don't let her get to you." While sincere and supportive, his words couldn't entirely quell the insidious voice of self-doubt that continued to whisper its toxic message.

His attempts to distract me often failed. Fleeting moments of panic, moments where fear resurfaced, reminding me of the looming competition and failure, interrupted even the most engaging conversations. The relentless pressure of internal and external expectations persisted, creating crushing weight.

One evening, while John helped me clean Apollo's tack, Karen sauntered by, her eyes lingering on us with an unsettling intensity. "Spending all your time with your boyfriend instead of training?" she sneers, her voice laced with a venomous undertone. "Maybe you should focus on the competition instead of romantic distractions."

John's hand tightened on mine. He looked at Karen, his expression a blend of anger and protective determination. "Jammie is more than capable, Karen. You don't have to worry about her." His response was a quiet assertion of support, a clear sign he would no longer tolerate her harassment. She taunted not only me; Karen laughs, a harsh, brittle sound that sends shivers down my spine. "We'll see about that," she says, her eyes gleaming with a malevolent intent. Then she turned and walked away, leaving us in the unsettling silence, the air thick with unspoken tension.

That night, I couldn't sleep. John held me close, his presence a source of comfort amidst the swirling anxieties. He whispered, his words creating a protective bubble around me. He reminded me again of my strength, talent, and resilience. But his unwavering belief in me felt like a comforting shield against the relentless barrage of Karen's taunts.

The days that followed were a blur of anxiety and preparation. The shadow of Karen's intimidation hung over every training session, over every moment spent in the stables, a constant, oppressive presence that weighed heavily on my mind. Still, John was my silent support, a quiet strength in the background. Yet, despite his constant reassurance, the internal battle raged on—a battle between self-doubt and the burgeoning self-belief that was emerging. The competition loomed, a daunting yet unavoidable challenge, a trial that shaped me, revealing a courage I didn't know I possessed. The Grand Prix transcended competition.

Chapter 8: Seeking Support from Friends

The scent of freshly baked cookies and the low hum of conversation offered a welcome change from the tense atmosphere of the stables. Sarah's living room, usually a whirlwind of teenage chaos, felt surprisingly calm that evening. Scattered cushions and blankets created a comfortable haven, starkly contrasting the rigid formality of the Grand Prix preparations. Ever the pragmatist, Sarah had organized a "chill-out" session, a much-needed break from the mounting pressure. Besides, Sarah, Emily, and Chloe were my closest friends since elementary school; their presence was a comforting balm to my frayed nerves.

"So," Sarah began, her voice soft, breaking the comfortable silence, "spill it. What's eating you?"

I hesitated, and my anxieties suddenly felt heavier than ever. The casual setting almost felt deceptive, a fragile bubble shielding me from the storm of self-doubt that raged within. Karen's taunts, the relentless pressure, and the fear of failure all threatened to overwhelm me. My friends' faces, etched with genuine concern, triggered my breakdown.

Trembling at first, I confessed my fears, my voice growing stronger as I spoke. I described how Karen constantly harassed me, subtly sabotaged my work, and appeared to enjoy my distress. I described my sleepless nights, constant anxiety, and crippling self-doubt.

The comfortable atmosphere shifted as I spoke, the lighthearted chatter replaced by a quiet intensity. My friends listened intently, their eyes filled with empathy and understanding. There were no interruptions, no trivializations. They allowed me to speak, letting my emotions flow freely, and offered a safe space where they accepted my vulnerability.

Emily, usually the most effervescent of the group, reached out and squeezed my hand. Her touch was gentle, a silent expression of support. "Jammie," she whispers, her voice laced with a quiet strength, "you're amazing. You're one of the most talented riders I know. Karen's intimidated. She fears you."

Chloe, our group's quiet observer, says thoughtfully, "It's not about your talent, Jammie. It's about her insecurities. She's trying to undermine your confidence because she fears losing."

Sarah, ever practical, offered a different perspective. "Look," she says, her tone firm but reassuring, "we all feel pressure. It's part of competing. But Karen's behavior is unacceptable. It's bullying. And you don't deserve that."

Their words, though simple, resonated deeply, chipping away at the wall of self-doubt I had built around myself. They weren't simply offering platitudes; they were providing a different lens through which to view my struggles. Their belief in me, their understanding, and their unwavering support felt like a lifeline in a sea of anxiety.

The conversation flowed naturally, moving from my anxieties to strategies for dealing with Karen. Emily discreetly suggested documenting Karen's actions should they escalate further. Chloe offered to be my "wing-woman" at the stables, a silent presence to deter Karen's more overt acts of intimidation. Ever the planner, Sarah even suggests that we develop a "mental resilience" plan — a series of coping mechanisms to manage stress and anxiety during the competition.

We spent hours talking, sharing experiences, offering advice, and reminding each other that we were stronger together. Their support went beyond words; it was a tangible thing, a tangible manifestation of friendship, a feeling of belonging, a shared understanding of the pressures and expectations that weighed heavily upon us. The casual setting shifted from a place of worry into a haven, a sanctuary where we could be honest and vulnerable, our friendship becoming a source of emotional and mental strength.

The cookies, initially a mere afterthought, became a symbol of our shared comfort and resilience. We laughed, cried, and shared stories about our struggles and fears of failure. It wasn't about the upcoming competition; it was about the strength of our friendship — a bond forged over years of shared experiences that gave me the strength I needed to face the challenges ahead.

Their unwavering belief in my abilities transcended the realm of equestrian sports. It served as a testament to the power of friendship, a support system that bolstered my confidence, and a constant source of encouragement during self-doubt. Their presence was a comforting counterpoint to the intensity of the competition, offering a much-needed sense of normalcy amid the chaos.

As the evening drew close, calm settled over me. The fear hadn't entirely vanished, but it felt less overwhelming, less suffocating. I left Sarah's house feeling lighter, stronger, and more equipped to face the challenges ahead. The impending Grand Prix still loomed, but it no longer felt insurmountable. I had my friends, the support system, and the anchor in the storm.

The next few days passed in a flurry of preparations. The atmosphere at the stables remained tense, Karen's presence still a constant source of anxiety. But now, I had a different perspective. I approached my training with renewed focus, each exercise a step towards proving my abilities to Karen and myself. I felt a growing sense of confidence, not the arrogant bravado Karen possessed, but a quiet strength rooted in self-belief and bolstered by the unwavering support of my friends.

Chloe's subtle presence near my stall served as a silent reassurance, deterring Karen's more blatant acts of aggression. Though not yet used, Emily's meticulous notes on Karen's behavior provided control and preparedness should things escalate. Sarah's "mental resilience plan" helped me structure my thoughts, focus on the present, and quiet the insidious voice of self-doubt.

I practiced deep breathing exercises, visualized my routine, focused on the connection with Apollo, and blocked out Karen's taunts, noise, distractions, and constant presence. I practiced visualizing success, not the perfect execution of my dressage routine, but also the feeling of accomplishment, pride in my performance, and recognition of my skill.

John, too, remained a constant source of support. He would meet me at the stables after my training, patiently listening to my anxieties, offering encouragement, and helping me to unwind. His presence was a quiet assurance, a testament to his unwavering belief in me, and his love a tangible shield against the storm of doubts. He understood the pressure, the expectations, and the relentless pursuit of excellence, and he offered his steady support without ever minimizing my struggles. He reminded me that the outcome of a single competition didn't determine my worth. Through my dedication, resilience, and powerful character, I faced adversity.

The day of the Grand Prix arrived, and though a tremor of anxiety remained, a newfound sense of calm, a quiet confidence that emanated from within, overshadowed it. I was prepared. Not only in my training, but also in my mental fortitude, emotional resilience, and unwavering support of my friends and boyfriend. The competition wouldn't be easy, but I was ready. I prepared to confront Karen, the judges, and myself. The journey had been challenging, fraught with self-doubt and intimidation. Still, it had also revealed a strength I never knew I possessed—a resilience forged in the fires of adversity—and a profound, unwavering belief in myself. I was ready.

Chapter 9: A Training Mishap

The crisp fall air bit at my cheeks as I mounted Apollo; his warm breath contrasted with the chill. The Grand Prix loomed, a menacing shadow eclipsing the vibrant fall foliage surrounding the stables. My carefully constructed calm — the fragile peace forged in the crucible of Sarah's living room — felt increasingly precarious. Each day felt like a tightrope, the balance between hope and fear, a delicate dance constantly threatened by the slightest misstep.

Today's training session began like any other. Sensing my nervousness, Apollo showed some restlessness. We started with the basics, the familiar movements, a soothing rhythm to quell the anxieties churning within me. The familiar pirouettes, the graceful passage, the collected walk—each exercise a minor victory against the rising tide of doubt. I felt a renewed sense of control, the careful choreography of our movements, and a bulwark against the storm of emotions threatening to engulf me.

Then came the piaffe. This notoriously demanding movement, requiring precise balance, strength, and timing, has always been both my greatest strength and my most significant source of anxiety. It demanded a deep connection between horse and rider, a harmonious melding of minds and bodies, a shared understanding that transcended the mere mechanics of movement. And today, that connection wavered.

Sensing my underlying tension, Apollo shifted his weight slightly, his usually unwavering rhythm faltering. A tiny, almost imperceptible hesitation, but enough to throw me off balance. My attempt to regain control failed; the precarious equilibrium shattered. Apollo stumbled, his front legs buckling slightly before he righted himself. A jolt of pain shot up my leg from the impact, and a wave of nausea followed.

For a moment, the world seemed to spin. Pain and fear combined in a sharp cry that I couldn't help but make. His controlled exterior collapsed, unveiling the hidden insecurity within. The training arena swam before my tear-blurred vision.

Apollo waited patiently, his big, dark eyes showing his worry. Sensing my distress, his soft nose nudged my hand. A silence so profound and complete descended that it felt as if the very air itself was heavy with an almost painful lack of sound. Frantic beating of my heart and shallow gasps for air were the only sounds I could hear, and they filled my ears with a deafening silence. The searing pain in my leg was excruciating.

In retrospect, all the painstaking work, endless hours of practice, and relentless pursuit of perfection I undertook seemed a colossal waste of time and energy. I was unsuccessful in my endeavors. My piaffe was far from perfect, and to make matters worse, I lost my composure after a slight error. I pictured Karen's smug face, her triumphant smirk mocking my despair.

Mr. Davies, my trainer, rushed over, his face etched with concern.

He dismounted me gently, his hands steady and reassuring. He examined my leg, and his touch was both gentle and thorough. The pain was real, sharp, and throbbing, a stark reminder of my vulnerability.

"It's a bruise, Jammie," he says, his voice soothing, Dressage through the fog of despair. "Apollo's fine too. It happens. Even the best riders have their off days." Despite their simplicity, his words offered a small measure of solace, a fragile raft in the turbulent sea of my emotions. His calm and reassuring manner helped quiet the storm raging within me; his presence was a steady anchor against the relentless waves of self-doubt.

"But...I'm supposed to be ready for the Grand Prix," I stammer, my voice trembling. "What if this happens again? What if I fail?"

Mr. Davies kneeled beside me, his gaze steady and unwavering. He understood my burden; self-imposed pressure, not familial. He understood the vulnerability that the fall had exposed, the fragility of my carefully constructed confidence.

"Jammie," he whispers, his voice laced with empathy, "you're a talented rider. One minor mishap doesn't change that. This highlights this sport's unpredictability, not your abilities. Setbacks happen; it's fine. What matters is how you respond."

He explains the incident was likely because of a combination of factors—Apollo's slight restlessness, my underlying anxiety, and perhaps a slight imbalance in my posture. He gently corrected my posture and guided me through a series of stretching exercises to release the tension in my leg and improve my balance.

Rather than simply dismissing my fear, he cleverly reframed it, skillfully redirecting my attention toward the aspects within my control—namely, maintaining a strong posture, regulating my breathing, and strengthening my connection with Apollo, my loyal companion. In his remarks, he underscored three key elements: the importance of cultivating mindfulness and self-awareness, the skill of recognizing Apollo's nuanced signals, and the absolute necessity of maintaining a state of mental readiness.

Helped me analyze the piaffe by breaking it down into its constituent parts, emphasizing the importance of precise timing, subtle shifts in weight, and nuanced communication between horse and rider. He spent the rest of the session helping me regain my confidence, gently guiding Apollo and me through the movements and building our trust and coordination.

A new calm settled over me as the sun dipped below the horizon, casting long shadows across the training arena. It wasn't the fragile calm of the previous days, but a stronger, more resilient sense of peace. The fall had shaken my confidence and exposed my vulnerability, but it had also served as a valuable lesson. It had reminded me of the importance of resilience, the need to learn from mistakes, and the crucial role of mental strength in equestrian sports.

The mishap wasn't a failure; it was a learning experience, a chance to refine my skills, to strengthen my bond with Apollo, and to solidify my mental resilience.

The Grand Prix still loomed, but the fear no longer felt insurmountable. I was ready. Not physically, but mentally and emotionally. Although painful, the fall strengthened me, forging a deeper connection with Apollo and renewing my faith in my abilities.

Chapter 10: Confronting her Fears

The next few days were a blur of intense preparation, a whirlwind of physical training interspersed with moments of quiet introspection. The physical aspect was familiar territory; I had spent hours honing my skills alongside Apollo, perfecting the intricate movements of the Grand Prix freestyle. But the mental preparation proved far more challenging; a relentless battle against the insidious whispers of self-doubt still echoed in my mind. The fall, though seemingly insignificant in the grand scheme of things, had exposed a deep-seated vulnerability, a crack in the carefully constructed armor of my confidence.

I spent hours alone in the stables, not riding, but simply sitting with Apollo, our quiet companionship a balm to my frayed nerves. His steady presence and unwavering trust were a grounding force, a constant reassurance amidst the turmoil. I would run my fingers through his silken mane, feeling the strength beneath his sleek coat, the power within his muscled frame. He was my constant in a chaotic world.

I employed visualization techniques, mentally rehearsing the Grand Prix routine and replaying each movement in my mind, perfecting the transitions, and ensuring harmony between horse and rider. I imagined the arena, the expectant crowd, the judging panel. Still, instead of focusing on the potential for failure, I visualized myself executing a flawless performance, Apollo responding to my every cue with effortless grace and precision. I saw myself as I felt confident and in control, with my movements fluid, elegant, and powerful. I replaced the image of Karen's smug face with the vision of my satisfied smile. This mental rehearsal became a ritual, a nightly exercise designed to instill confidence and banish fear.

It wasn't easy. Doubt still crept in, whispering insidious lies in the quiet moments I battled these intrusive thoughts, fighting back with affirmations of my skill, strength, and resilience. I reminded myself of the countless hours of training, the dedication, the sacrifices, the unwavering support of my family and friends, and, most importantly, the unyielding trust of Apollo.

One evening, while watching the sunset paint the sky in fiery hues of orange and crimson, I realized that my fear wasn't about failure in the Grand Prix. The legacy of past generations of champion riders weighed heavily upon my shoulders, an invisible burden that threatened to crush me. I always aimed for perfection, motivated by a desire to prove myself to the ones I cared about and looked up to. But I lost sight of the joy and pure passion for the sport that had initially ignited my love for horses.

This realization was a turning point. I shifted my focus, re-centering my priorities consciously. The Grand Prix was no longer a competition, a test of skill; it became an opportunity to celebrate my love for horses, express myself through the beautiful art of dressage, and forge a deeper connection with Apollo. I rode passionately, joyfully, completely present, purely for the love of it, whatever the result.

This new perspective was liberating. It didn't erase my fear, but it transformed it, tempering its intensity, stripping away its power to paralyze me. I viewed the Grand Prix not as a threat, but as a challenge — a test of my mettle, an opportunity to push my limits and discover my true potential.

My training sessions took on an extra dimension. The focus shifted from the relentless pursuit of perfection to a conscious effort to connect with Apollo on a deeper level. I learned to listen to his subtle cues, anticipate his needs, and read his emotions. Our communication became more intuitive and harmonious, a silent conversation transcending words. We were no longer horse and rider; we were a team, two beings working in perfect synchronicity, united by a common purpose.

Mindfulness practices, focusing on my breath and grounding myself in the present, helped silence my mind's incessant chatter. I practiced deep breathing exercises, learning to calm my racing heart and steady my nerves. I also meditated, seeking a quiet space within myself, a place of peace and tranquility that allowed me to connect with my inner strength. These practices helped to build my mental resilience, equipping me with the tools to navigate the challenges ahead.

John, my boyfriend, was a constant source of support throughout this challenging period. He understood my fears, my anxieties, and the immense pressure I was under. He never dismissed my concerns, but reminded me of my strength, talent, and resilience. His unwavering belief in me was a source of comfort, a steady anchor amidst the storms of self-doubt. He listened patiently to my anxieties, offering encouragement, reassurance, and practical advice. His presence helped me maintain perspective, see the bigger picture, and remember that the Grand Prix was one competition, one chapter in a much longer story.

The evening before the Grand Prix, I sat with Apollo in the stables; the silence broken only by the gentle rustle of hay and the soft whinny of the nearby horses. I brushed his coat, feeling the smoothness of his skin, the warmth of his body. His presence was reassuring, his trust palpable. I looked into his dark eyes, and in that moment, I felt an overwhelming sense of calm, a profound connection that transcended words. All my anxieties and doubts seemed to melt away, replaced by a deep understanding of gratitude and peace.

I knew I was ready. Not because I had banished all my fears, but because I had learned to embrace them, to accept my vulnerabilities, to approach the Grand Prix not with a desperate need to prove myself, but with a profound love for the sport, a deep respect for Apollo, and a quiet confidence in my abilities. The Grand Prix loomed as a monumental challenge, but I felt a newfound strength and resilient determination to face whatever came my way.

This was not about winning; it was about embracing the journey, pushing my limits, celebrating the bond between horse and rider, and finding my true self in the competition's heart. The outcome was uncertain, but I knew I would ride with passion, grace, courage, and love for myself and Apollo. This was my moment.

Chapter 11: Arrival at the Grand Prix Venue

The air crackled with anticipation as the Grand Prix venue unfolded before me. It wasn't a place; it was a living organism, a symphony of sights and sounds that both thrilled and terrified. The sprawling complex hummed with a frenetic energy, a kaleidoscope of activity that swirled around me like a dizzying vortex. Horses, sleek and powerful, were being led into their stables, their coats gleaming under the bright morning sun. The rhythmic clip-clop of hooves on the paved pathways created a constant, almost hypnotic soundtrack to the scene. Trainers, their faces etched with hope and anxiety, scurried around, issuing last-minute instructions, their voices a cacophony of commands and encouragement. The scent of hay, leather, and horse sweat hung heavy in the air, a heady perfume that invigorated and unsettled me.

My horse, Apollo, remained remarkably calm amidst the chaos. He stood quietly in his trailer, his dark eyes reflecting the bustling activity around him. His steady presence was my anchor, grounding me amid this whirlwind of excitement and nerves. I brushed his soft, silken coat as I approached his trailer, feeling the familiar strength beneath his muscular frame. He nudged my hand with his velvety nose, a silent gesture of reassurance, a tacit acknowledgment of our shared journey.

The atmosphere in the stables was palpable, a strange mixture of intense concentration and nervous energy. Riders moved with a focused intensity, their movements precise, efficient, and almost robotic in their precision. The air crackled with unspoken tension, a silent battle of wills that transcended the physical realm. I could feel the weight of expectations, the pressure to perform, pressing down upon me like a heavy cloak. I saw Karen, my rival, effortlessly elegant as she worked with her horse, her confident demeanor radiating an almost arrogant self-assurance. Her presence seemed to amplify my anxieties, a stark reminder of the challenge ahead.

I felt my nervous energy resonate with the frantic heartbeat and relentless rhythm of the venue. My sweat-slick hands felt clammy. My breath hitched in my throat, a tight knot of apprehension constricting my chest. I tried to breathe deeply, center myself, and find the inner calm I had cultivated over the past few days.

But the nervousness clung to me, tenacious, whispering doubts and fears into my ear. "What if you don't succeed?" it hisses. "Disappointing everyone is a possibility, what then? What if you let Apollo down?"

Seeking a refuge from the outside world, I closed my eyes, hoping to find solace and peace in the stillness and quietude of my mind. As I replayed my visualization exercises in my mind, the images of a flawless performance danced behind my eyelids, a vivid and persistent reminder of my goals. My vision was of myself riding with effortless grace, precision, and power. In my mind, Apollo flawlessly followed my cues, his movements fluid and his energy both vibrant and controlled. The judges' appreciative expressions mirrored my own feelings of achievement. Swapping Karen's smug smile for my own satisfied grin felt like conquering not just my rival, but also my inner turmoil.

The feeling of panic gradually subsided, giving way to a growing sense of resolve. I took a deep breath, exhaled slowly, and opened my eyes, my gaze meeting Apollo's. In his dark, intelligent eyes, I saw unwavering trust and support. His presence was a balm to my frayed nerves, a tangible reminder of our shared bond and the journey we had taken together. He was my anchor, partner, and friend, and in that moment, I felt a renewed sense of confidence, a quiet strength that settled deep within my core.

The preparations for the Grand Prix were meticulous and intense. The grooming of Apollo was a ritualistic process; each stroke of the brush was a gesture of respect, a demonstration of my commitment to our shared success. His coat gleamed like polished ebony, his muscles rippling beneath his sleek skin. I checked and re-checked his tack, ensuring everything was in perfect order and that nothing would compromise our performance. I scrutinized every detail with meticulous care, no matter how seemingly insignificant. Anticipation vibrated, a palpable tension filling the stable.

The anticipation was almost unbearable. The waiting felt like an eternity, and each clock ticked, echoing in the stillness. Riders paced, trainers offered final words of encouragement, and the sound of hooves on the ground was a constant reminder of the imminent commencement of the competition. My heart pounded against my ribs like a trapped bird, a frantic rhythm that mirrored my own rising anxiety. I took another deep breath, trying to center myself, to calm the storm within my chest. I needed to focus, concentrate, and prepare myself for the challenge ahead.

The mounting nervousness was a physical entity, a heavy weight pressing down my chest, constricting my breath. My legs felt shaky, and my hands trembled slightly. Doubt crept in, insidious and persistent, whispering its venomous lies into my ear. But I fought back, reminding myself of all the hours of training, the dedication, the sacrifices. My family, friends, and especially Apollo's unwavering trust came to mind; their support was constant. I focused on the positive, visualizing success, replaying the flawless routine. I repeated my affirmations, my mantra of strength and resilience, until the negativity faded, replaced by a quiet determination.

The waiting was agony. Time seemed endless; competitors constantly entered and left the arena. The atmosphere was thick with tension, a palpable energy that filled every corner of the stable. I tried to engage in mindfulness exercises, focusing on my breath and centering myself in the present moment. But the anxiety remained, a persistent hum beneath the surface, a constant reminder of the challenge ahead. I needed to calm my nerves and channel the energy into a positive force. The time had come. My name was called.

The dreaded, longed-for moment arrived. It was time to enter the arena. As I led Apollo towards the gate, adrenaline coursed through my veins, a heady mix of fear and excitement. The crowd roared, a wave of sound that washed over me, almost knocking me off balance. The arena's bright lights were blinding, the vastness of the space overwhelming. But as I looked at Apollo, his dark eyes calm, I found my strength again. This wasn't about the Grand Prix; it was about us, our journey, and our bond.

Chapter 12: Meeting Other Competitors

It felt like traversing a minefield, walking to the rider's lounge. A palpable tension, like a low thrumming baseline, punctuated every step from other competitors, adding to their nervous energy. The lounge was a study in contrasts—a space where camaraderie and rivalry existed in an uneasy equilibrium. Riders, some meticulously grooming their horses' tack, others huddled in anxious groups, their conversations a hushed murmur of strategizing and anxieties. The aroma of expensive leather, polished boots, and strong coffee hung heavy, a potent blend of the mundane and the extraordinary.

My eyes fell upon a group clustered near a window overlooking the arena. Among them was a girl with fiery red hair, pulled back into a severe ponytail, her face a mask of fierce concentration. She meticulously cleaned her boots, the rhythmic swish of the cloth a counterpoint to the nervous energy around her. Her horse, a striking chestnut with a blaze of white down its face, stood patiently nearby, its head lowered, sensing the tension in its rider. There was an aura of quiet intensity about her, a palpable sense that she meant business. She looked like a seasoned competitor who had navigated these high-stakes arenas before. I wondered about her, picturing her flawless routine, her unwavering composure under pressure, her drive to succeed.

Another rider caught my eye—a lanky young man with tousled blond hair and an easygoing smile that belied the steely glint in his eyes. He casually chats with friends, his laughter echoing through the lounge, seeming remarkably relaxed given the circumstances. Yet, beneath his affable demeanor, I sensed a quiet confidence, a subtle air of self-assurance. His horse, a powerful black stallion, stood nearby, its muscular frame a testament to its power and strength. The man's apparent casualness was deceptive, I thought. Beneath the laid-back charm lay a deep-seated competitiveness, a burning desire to prove his mettle. He was a dark horse in every sense of the word.

Then I saw her—Isabelle Moreau, the reigning national champion.

An entourage of admirers surrounded her, observing her every movement and analyzing her every word. Her presence exuded an almost ethereal grace, a regal bearing that commanded attention. She was undeniably talented, with a reputation that preceded her. Her composure was astonishing, a stark contrast to the nervous energy surrounding her. She spoke with a quiet authority, her words carrying a weight that reflected her experience and skill. Her magnificent gray mare stood nearby, its elegant movements betraying the power beneath its graceful exterior.

Isabelle epitomized refinement and poise, a picture of effortless elegance. The others seemed to orbit her, drawn to her aura of success. I couldn't help but feel a surge of both admiration and apprehension.

There was a palpable buzz around another rider, a slight, unassuming girl named Chloe. A quiet intensity emanated from her, a focused energy clear in every meticulous detail of her preparation. Her elegant mare, though delicately built, possessed a quiet strength, unlike some others. Chloe's interactions with her horse were incredibly gentle yet firm, her touch light yet commanding. She seemed to speak a language only they understood, a silent conversation of trust and understanding. I sensed an unwavering dedication in her, a fierce determination that belied her quiet demeanor. She wasn't aiming for flashy displays, but precise execution and a connection with her horse — a calm strength that was equally interesting.

In contrast, a group of boisterous riders filled the space with laughter and loud conversation, breaking through the quiet intensity of the others. Their banter brimmed with inside jokes and shared memories, yet beneath the lighthearted surface was a strong sense of team spirit and a commitment to lifting one another up. Their horses, a diverse collection of breeds and sizes, were equally boisterous, their energy infectious. They seemed less focused on individual glory and more on the camaraderie of the sport, their collective energy creating a positive, supportive atmosphere. Their energy was contagious; friendship and support thrived, despite fierce competition.

Observing these diverse individuals, their varied approaches to the competition, and their complex relationships with their horses, I felt awe and intimidation. Each rider possessed a unique personality, and each horse had a distinctive character. The differences highlighted the multifaceted nature of equestrian sports and the diverse approaches to achieving success. However, the shared passion for their mounts was a constant—a thread of unity binding them together in a competitive yet supportive environment. This wasn't a competition; it was a vibrant tapestry woven with threads of talent, determination, anxiety, and an unwavering love for their equine partners.

The sheer variety of approaches was striking. Some riders seemed to be fueled by an intense internal drive, their focus entirely on their performance, their movements precise and calculated. Others radiated a calm confidence, their interactions with their horses suggesting years of seamless partnership. Still others operated in a supportive, collaborative mode, sharing tips and encouraging one another, their relationships with their horses deeply affectionate.

The atmosphere in the lounge was a strange cocktail of intense competition and surprising camaraderie. Riders helped each other, shared advice, and offered encouragement, even amidst the inherent rivalry. It was a complex dance of ambition, fair play, rivalry, and respect. Watching this equestrian world, I felt excited and apprehensive. The Grand Prix loomed, a monumental challenge that would test my riding skills and mental fortitude. The encounter with these other competitors was a powerful reminder of the high stakes, intense competition, and incredible talent showcased at this elite level. It also served as a reassuring confirmation that I wasn't alone, that others shared my passion, my anxieties, and my unwavering dedication to the art of dressage.

This journey wasn't simply my own; it was part of a larger story, a collective narrative woven together by the shared threads of passion, ambition, and the unbreakable bond between horse and rider. As the moment of truth approached, I felt a new resolve, quiet determination, and a strengthened sense of belonging within this unique community. The competition would be fierce, but I was ready. I prepared to face every competitor, including Karen, Isabelle, and, most importantly, myself.

Chapter 13: The Opening Ceremony

The air crackled; the electricity felt unrelated to fall's crispness. It was the collective breath of hundreds of spectators, the nervous energy emanating from the riders themselves, a tangible hum that vibrated through the ground beneath my feet. The opening ceremony of the Grand Prix was about to begin.

The dazzling lights transformed the arena. Around the perimeter, flags of various nations fluttered in the gentle breeze, creating a vibrant tapestry of colors against the backdrop of the majestic stands, which overflowed with spectators. The sounds were a symphony of anticipation—the hushed whispers of the crowd, the rhythmic clip-clop of horses' hooves echoing from the stables, and the occasional burst of excited chatter.

Silence gripped the crowd; the announcer's booming voice resonated. He spoke of tradition, the history of the Grand Prix, and the dedication and skill required to compete at such a high level. He carefully chose his words to build suspense, underscore the weight of this moment, and create an atmosphere thick with expectation.

The national anthem played a stirring melody that seemed to swell with the rising tide of anticipation. The flags rose high, the colors vibrant under the spotlight, representing the nations whose riders had traveled far and wide to compete in this prestigious competition. Each flag represented countless hours of training, countless sacrifices made by both rider and horse. Despite the intense rivalry, the shared passion that united these competitors was palpable in the moment of patriotic pride they shared.

Then, the riders entered—one by one; they rode into the arena, each pair a study in contrasts. There was Isabelle Moreau, her gray mare moving with an almost supernatural grace, her presence radiating confidence and regal poise. As she passed, the crowd erupted in thunderous applause, her flawless performance setting incredibly high expectations.

Karen, my rival, rode in with an air of haughty confidence. Her chestnut stallion pranced with an almost arrogant grace, mirroring her attitude. Her eyes, sharp and focused, seemed to pierce through the crowd, a silent declaration of intent.

With her small, elegant mare, Chloe entered with quiet dignity, her focus absolute. The bond between her and her horse was clear in their synchronized movements, a testament to their years of training.

Even the boisterous group of riders from the previous day displayed controlled excitement. Focused intensity had muted their laughter and chatter. The support and camaraderie within their group were visible; they shared quiet nods of encouragement, their presence a cohesive force.

I watched them all with a growing mixture of awe and nervousness.

This wasn't a competition; it was a display of human and equine excellence, a testament to the dedication, the skill, and the unwavering bond between horse and rider. The ceremony marked not a beginning;

As I entered the arena, my horse, Comet, responded to the event's energy with a nervous energy of his own. His breathing grew deeper, his powerful muscles tensing beneath my touch. I felt his anxiety mirrored in my heart, a mixture of excitement and terror that made my hands clammy. The roar of the crowd, the flashing lights, the magnitude of the event—it all threatened to overwhelm me.

Comet's gaze sharpened my attention. His trust in me, his silent reliance, helped me calm my nerves. His quiet strength reassured me, and the feeling of his warm breath against my cheek was a physical anchor in this storm of excitement. Focusing on my connection with him melted away the collective energy, expectations, and pressures.

A living thing, anticipation throbbed palpably in the air. The hushed expectancy of the crowd amplified every rustle, every cough, every shifted foot. It felt like time had slowed, each second stretching out, each heartbeat echoing loudly in the sudden silence. It was a moment suspended between the past and the future, a brief pause before the storm of the competition broke loose. The grandeur of the stadium, the disciplined precision of the horses, and the nervous excitement of the riders combined to create a breathtaking spectacle.

I felt a deep breath escape my lips, a moment of vulnerability instantly overshadowed by a surge of resolute determination. That was the end. The weight of expectations, the pressure from my family, and the rivalry with Karen dissipated, replaced by an unwavering focus on the connection with my horse.

The comet moved beneath me with quiet power and sensitivity that reflected my shifting emotions. He sensed my change in demeanor, my growing focus and determination, and responded kindly. The anxiety dissipated, replaced by a calm partnership, a quiet understanding transcending words.

We were ready. The opening ceremony was over, and now it was our turn. The Grand Prix had truly begun. I felt ready, finally. I am not technically prepared, but I am ready in my heart and soul, prepared to face the challenge ahead, to give my all, and to discover my true potential.

Chapter 14: First Round Performance

The announcer's voice, crisp and clear, called my name. My heart hammered against my ribs, a frantic drumbeat against the otherwise serene calm of the arena. Sensing my tension shift, Comet shifted slightly beneath me, his breath warm against my leg. I took a deep breath, trying to steady my racing pulse, and gently squeezed his neck, offering a silent reassurance. He responded with a soft nuzzle against my shoulder, a gesture of unwavering trust that settled my nerves. This wasn't about the competition, but the partnership we shared — a silent conversation woven through years of training and mutual understanding.

Entering the arena felt like stepping onto a stage, bathed in the intense glare of spotlights. Silence reigned, punctuated only by rare coughs or rustling. Thousands of eyes were upon us, each pair a silent judge, and the weight of their expectation pressed down on me. But then, as I focused on Comet's rhythmic breathing, the pressure lessened. His presence was my anchor, the steadying force that grounded me in the moment's storm.

Our test began with the extended trot, a test of our suppleness and control. Comet responded brilliantly, his gait smooth and powerful, and his movements were a testament to the years of meticulous training we had invested in him. I felt the subtle shift in his weight, the effortless response to my aids, the harmonious flow of our movements. Each stride was a silent conversation, a seamless interplay between horse and rider. He moved with a grace that belied his powerful physique, his body seemingly weightless despite his immense strength. I adjusted my position, subtly guiding him, and felt the responsive tension and relaxation of his muscles — a delicate dance of mutual understanding.

The rhythmic beat of Comet's hooves punctuated the collective stillness of the arena only on the soft ground, a metronome marking the measured precision of our performance.

As we transitioned into the passage, after a moment of delicate balance and refined movement, I focused on maintaining the rhythmic flow. Comet's movements became more collected, almost ethereal. His controlled power was apparent in his measured and precise strides and restrained energy. The passage required strength, precision, and an almost supernatural lightness — a ballet of controlled energy. It was a testament to the years spent honing our skills — a delicate symphony of movements that required perfect synchronization. Any hesitation or interruption in the flow could derail our performance. The air crackled with expectation, and each step felt like a tightrope between success and failure.

The piaffe, a demonstration of exceptional balance and control, further tested our limits. The rhythmic beat of Comet's hooves echoed in the hushed arena, each step a testament to his powerful muscles and incredible balance. Held himself poised, not moving an inch from the center of the arena, an embodiment of graceful power. The rhythm had to be unwavering, the precision impeccable. Any disruption, no matter how slight, would be glaringly apparent to the judges, breaking the spell of controlled energy. And with each beat of his powerful legs, his body expressing a quiet strength clear in his steady gaze and unwavering balance, I felt a deep sense of pride and partnership.

The one-tempo changes proved to be a highlight. The transitions between walk and trot were fluid and precise, almost magical, the changes in gait seamless and swift. Comet responded to my slightest cues, each change a testament to the deep understanding we had cultivated over years of training. His movements were precise and powerful, a display of athleticism and grace that captivated the crowd. The elegant precision of his steps was nothing short of breathtaking; each transition felt like a seamless wave of motion, a perfect exchange between our bodies and spirits.

However, amidst the beauty and precision of our performance, a flicker of anxiety still lingered. During an intricate series of transitions, a hint of tension crept into Comet's movements in a moment of heightened pressure. He stumbled slightly during a transition from piaffe to passage, a slight misstep, nearly imperceptible to the untrained eye, but a clear sign to me of the pressure we both felt. My heart skipped a beat; I could feel the judges' eyes upon us, scrutinizing every movement, every breath, every minute detail. For a moment, my self-doubt threatened to resurface, the pressure threatening to overwhelm us both. But then, I recalled the unwavering trust we shared and the connection we forged in the endless hours spent perfecting our skills. We experienced this moment together. With a renewed focus, I righted our course, guiding Comet with gentle yet firm commands, smoothing out the momentary lapse with a renewed intensity and precision.

Karen's performance followed, a stark contrast to my own. Her chestnut stallion, a magnificent beast, performed with a dazzling display of athleticism. His confident movements showcased a raw power that commanded respect and admiration. With her arrogant grace, Karen seemed to ride him like an extension of her own will, dominating the arena with an air of unwavering self-assurance.

She rode with an aggressive energy that starkly contrasted my more subtle approach, showcasing a confident, sometimes flashy style that resonated with the audience. Her performance was a breathtaking spectacle of equine athleticism, but lacked the refined elegance I strived for.

The judges' scores would ultimately determine our fate, but the experience itself was more than a competition; it was a testament to the years of dedication, the unwavering commitment, the silent communication between horse and rider. It was a story of trust, resilience, and growth, and in that moment, whatever the outcome, I felt accomplishment that transcended the final scores. I had faced my fears, overcome them, and given them my all.

It felt victorious, despite being only the first round. The actual test, however, remained. I felt prepared, despite the intensifying competitive pressure. I was prepared to face the challenge ahead and give my absolute best.

The final movements of our performance came, the graceful passage again showcasing his effortless grace, ending with a powerful, collected halt, his body still and powerful, as if frozen in a moment of perfect poise. The silence that followed was thick with anticipation, broken only by the rhythmic thudding of my heart. Then, a slow, measured applause broke through, growing louder and more resonant with every passing second. The relief was palpable.

As we exited the arena, I glanced back at Comet, his flanks glistening with sweat, his breath still slightly ragged, but his eyes were soft and calm. He had given me everything he had, and I had given him mine. Whatever the outcome, we had faced the challenge together, sharing a bond that transcended competition. The journey started; I felt quietly satisfied. The Grand Prix was a relentless test of skill and determination, and we were getting started. The upcoming rounds will be tougher, requiring increased skill, stamina, and nerve. But for now, I enjoyed the success of our first performance, eagerly expecting what's to come.

Chapter 15: Initial Reactions and Feedback

The hushed anticipation in the arena was almost unbearable as we left the ring. Comet, usually brimming with energy, walked with a quiet dignity, his breath coming in slightly ragged gasps. He knew, as well as I did, that our convincing performance wasn't flawless. That tiny stumble during the passage had been a blip in an otherwise stellar performance — a small crack in the carefully constructed façade of perfection. My legs felt like jelly, a strange mixture of exhaustion and exhilaration washing over me.

My trainer, Mr. Evans, was waiting for me, his face a mask of controlled emotion. He embraced me in a quick hug, his hand clapping my shoulder in a gesture of encouragement and analysis. "Well done, Jammie," he says, his voice low and calm. "A solid performance. A few minor corrections, but overall, impressive." The small reassurance was like a magical release to my raw nerves. Knowing I'd performed to the best of my ability, despite the stumble, gave me a measure of solace.

The immediate feedback from the judges was less comforting. While polite and professional, their comments included so much technical jargon that only a seasoned dressage rider could fully understand.

The judges praised Comet's power and my precision in specific movements, although they noted hesitation in the passage and a slight lack of fluidity in one pirouette. They emphasized the need for better control and precision, particularly under pressure. Though measured, their words conveyed an expectation of higher standards for the coming rounds.

Karen, her face a mask of practiced indifference, offered a curt nod and a thin-lipped, "Not bad," she passed me, her chestnut stallion pawing the ground impatiently. Her words, meant to sting, only confirmed the intensity of the rivalry. It fueled me strangely enough. Her apparent confidence was a facade. I could sense the tremor of insecurity beneath the veneer.

My parents' reaction was much more emotional. They rushed towards me, relief evident on their faces, mingled with pride and a hint of disappointment. My mother, ever the perfectionist, focused on the stumble, while my father, ever the supporter, celebrated our resilience. Their opposing reactions mirrored the conflicting emotions that churned within me. The pressure to live up to their legacy was immense, but their love and unwavering support were my anchors in the competition's storm.

John, my boyfriend, was waiting near the stables. He grabbed my hands, his eyes wide with admiration. He didn't focus on the technical aspects of the performance, but praised my courage and determination, utterly oblivious to the judge's critiques. "You were incredible, Jammie," he exclaims, his genuine enthusiasm a welcome counterpoint to the more measured feedback I'd received. His support centered him, highlighting the journey's importance over judging and competition.

The other riders offered a mixed bag of congratulations and subtle barbs. Some whispered their admiration for Comet's power, while others subtly pointed out the flaws in our performance. Each comment, though small, contributed to a growing sense of pressure. I replayed every movement in my head, analyzing every transition, every subtle shift in Comet's weight, and every twitch of his ear. The self-doubt, a constant companion, crept back in.

The hours that followed were a blur of activity. Limited time remained to consider previous errors as the next rounds drew near. I spent the afternoon meticulously grooming Comet, scrubbing away the sweat and grime of the first performance. I spoke to him quietly, reassuring him, apologizing for the stumble, and reaffirming our bond. He nuzzled his head against my chest, his soft breaths mirroring my need for calm.

Mr. Evans and I reviewed the judges' comments, dissecting each point with clinical precision. We identified areas for improvement, focusing on refining our transitions and enhancing our overall control. He was encouraging, patiently guiding me through corrective exercises. He focused on strengthening the areas where I had faltered, emphasizing the importance of maintaining a calm and confident demeanor throughout the performance. The rigorous training sessions required a level of focus and stamina that pushed us both to our limits.

The evening brought a brief respite. I spent some time with John, sharing my anxieties and concerns. He listened patiently, offering words of encouragement and support. His presence was a grounding influence, a reminder that I wasn't alone in this journey. We talked about the competition, our hopes and fears, the challenges we faced, and the triumphs we celebrated. In his gentle embrace, I found solace, a sanctuary from the relentless pressure. His unwavering support was a constant source of strength, reminding me that the scores did not solely define the accurate measure of success, but by the dedication, growth, and love found along the way.

The second round came faster than expected. The pressure increased to a level ten times greater than before, creating an immense and overwhelming force. My earlier slight stumble lingered in my thoughts, a persistent worry threatening to disrupt and distract my concentration completely. However, I am finding a newfound confidence and a stronger resolve is growing inside me. Round one's feedback, positive or negative, guided improvements. The support of my family, Mr. Evans, and John, provided stability, a grounding force against the swirling anxieties of the competition.

Entering the arena this time, I felt a renewed sense of purpose. I learned from my mistakes and was determined to showcase a performance that reflected my growth. The judges' critiques were constructive, highlighting areas where I needed improvement. I focused on refining those aspects during the training sessions, refining my transitions, and emphasizing precision and clarity. Comet responded to my renewed energy. He, too, had grown from the experiences of the first round, his steps more confident, his movements more fluent and powerful.

Throughout the performance, the quiet, steady strength that I had found in our partnership radiated outwards. I guided Comet, focusing on our shared journey, our silent communication. This time, the performance flowed seamlessly. With each movement, there was a noticeable increase in precision, power, and expressiveness, showcasing a logical progression in skill and artistry. The dancer performed a flawless piaffe. What was once anxiety-inducing tension between us has developed into a powerful, synchronized team effort.

As we concluded our performance, anticipation filled the silence. This time, the applause was stronger, more enthusiastic. I allowed myself to bask in the success before focusing on the following challenges. The judges' feedback was considerably more positive. They acknowledged the noticeable improvement in our control, timing, and harmony.

The judges praised our ability to rise above the pressure and execute our maneuvers flawlessly, showcasing skill and composure under the pressure of competition.

Despite the Grand Prix's continuation, the second round felt like a significant win. It wasn't about the scores, but about proving that I could overcome my fears, harness my insecurities, and perform to the best of my ability. Perseverance, our bond, unwavering support. These fueled my success. The journey had been challenging, filled with self-doubt and pressure. Still, amidst the anxieties, I had discovered the unwavering power of self-belief, and the unbreakable strength of the bond shared between a rider and their horse. The road ahead was still long, yet I approached it with a newfound clarity and a strengthened conviction. This wasn't a race; it was self-discovery. The third and final round was approaching, but there was no fear; this time, only quiet confidence, and a resolute determination to give everything to it.

Chapter 16: Increased Competition

With the third round, approaching, the air crackled with a strange energy. The initial excitement had settled into a simmering intensity, a palpable tension that hung heavy in the air of the stables. The camaraderie of the early days had fractured, replaced by a subtle yet pervasive rivalry — a silent battle for supremacy waged with carefully veiled glances and calculated maneuvers. Even the horses seemed to sense the shift. Their usual playful antics muted, their movements reflecting the heightened atmosphere. Comet, usually a whirlwind of playful energy, was quieter, more focused, sensing the shift in my demeanor.

I frayed my nerves. A fine wire stretched taut. While exhilarating, the initial victory in the second round hadn't erased the underlying anxiety. Instead, it had heightened the stakes, amplifying the pressure. The whispers, the subtle criticisms, the calculated displays of confidence from other riders—all contributed to a growing sense of unease.

Karen, in particular, had become more pronounced in her displays of arrogance. Her pre-performance routines were exaggerated, almost theatrical. She spent an inordinate amount of time grooming her stallion, each stroke a deliberate performance, each movement calculated to impress. Her casual conversations with other riders felt laced with subtle barbs; her laughter was slightly too loud, and her comments dripped with thinly veiled superiority. It was a calculated strategy, designed to unsettle her rivals, to sow seeds of doubt. I tried to ignore her, to focus solely on my preparation, but her presence was a constant, irritating hum in the background.

Sensing the heightened tension, the other competitors became increasingly guarded. Because of heightened tension, tense silence and careful avoidance of eye contact replaced the usual friendly banter. The stables, once a hive of social activity, now felt strangely isolated, each rider cocooned in their world of preparation and anxiety. The air was thick with unspoken competition, a silent war fought not with words but carefully executed maneuvers and steely gazes.

Even though Mr. Evans seemed more subdued, a quiet intensity replaced his usually jovial demeanor. He clearly understood the pressure and expectations I felt, leaving no room for misinterpretation. In our training sessions, he emphasized not only physical skill but also mental preparedness, particularly the importance of controlling my nerves and staying focused amidst the chaotic atmosphere of competition. To help me cope with the immense pressure of the final round, he patiently taught me a range of techniques, encompassing breathing exercises, visualization methods, and effective strategies for managing stress and anxiety.

The pressure wasn't coming from the competitors. My parents, while supportive, were also intensely focused on my performance. Their subtle anxieties, their occasional comments on the slightest imperfection, only amplified the pressure I already felt. They yearned for me to surpass their achievements and cement the family's legacy in the world of dressage. While born from love and admiration, their expectations felt like a heavy cloak, smothering my natural ability and joy. I battled my insecurities and the weight of their hopes and dreams.

John, thankfully, remained my constant source of support. He understood the pressures of the competition, even if he didn't fully grasp the intricacies of dressage. He didn't focus on the technical aspects of my performance; instead, he celebrated my courage, resilience, and dedication. His unwavering belief in me was a vital anchor, reminding me that my worth extended beyond the scores, the accolades, and the expectations of others. Helped me keep perspective, reminding me of the joy of riding, the bond I shared with Comet, and my sheer love for the sport.

Inevitably, the final day arrived. The arena was buzzing with energy, a volatile mix of anticipation and anxiety. The atmosphere was electric, charged with the collective tension of the riders and spectators. As I led Comet into the warm-up area, I could feel the weight of everyone's expectations pressing down on me. The other riders and their gleaming horses displayed impeccable turnout; their precise movements reflected a heightened sense of urgency and focus.

This wasn't a competition; it was a culmination of years of dedication, countless hours of training, and countless sacrifices. It was a test not of skill and talent, but of mental fortitude — of resilience and the unwavering spirit needed to thrive under intense pressure.

Winning mattered most, yet a dawning realization emerged: this surpassed mere victory. It was a journey of personal growth and an affirmation of my ability to overcome self-doubt.

Points weren't the victory; overcoming hardship was.

Karen's performance before mine felt like an intentional intimidation tactic. Her routine was flawless, a breathtaking display of skill and precision. The crowd roared its approval; the sound echoing in the arena, adding to the pressure I felt. Ignoring apprehension, I concentrated on breathing, Comet's gait, our unspoken connection.

Entering the arena, I felt a strange sense of calm. Determination, fierce and new, eclipsed lingering fear. This wasn't about winning; it was about proving to myself that I could overcome my fears, rise above the pressure, and perform to the best of my ability. The judges' scores were secondary to the personal victory I was striving for, a win over self-doubt and the weight of expectation.

The performance itself was a blur of motion. With Comet, I danced seamlessly, our movements and energy intertwined. Each transition was flawless, each pirouette executed with precision, each passage infused with emotion. The connection between us was palpable, an unspoken language that transcended words, a symphony of movement and grace.

As we concluded our performance, the silence that followed felt infinite, charged with unspoken judgment. Then, the applause erupted, a wave of sound that washed over me, a wave of relief and affirmation. It was the most powerful applause I had ever received, a testament to the extraordinary performance we had shared.

The judges' scores were high, exceeding even my expectations.

Success stemmed from personal growth, unwavering family support, and my bond with Comet, not merely statistics. The competition had intensified; and the pressure had been immense. Victory brought transformation; I am stronger, more confident, and surer of myself, both personally and professionally. The competition had been a crucible, forging a stronger, more resilient me.

Chapter 17: Strategies and Adjustments

The celebratory buzz of my victory in the third round quickly faded, replaced by the chilling realization that the Grand Prix final was only hours away. The pressure, once a manageable hum, had become a deafening roar. Karen's flawless and breathtaking performance had served as a stark reminder of the caliber of competition I faced. Her calculated arrogance and her theatrical displays weren't simply a personality quirk; they were deliberate strategies designed to unsettle and intimidate. I realized I needed to adapt, not my riding, but my entire approach to the competition.

My initial strategy, which focused solely on technical perfection, proved insufficient. I needed to incorporate mental resilience into my game plan. Mr. Evans, sensing my shift in demeanor, devoted our training sessions to honing my mental fortitude. He introduced me to mindfulness techniques, guiding me through breathing exercises designed to calm my racing heart and center my focus. We practiced visualization, mentally rehearsing my routine, anticipating potential challenges, and visualizing successful outcomes. It wasn't about ignoring the pressure; it was about learning to manage it and harness its energy, rather than being consumed by it.

He also emphasized the importance of self-compassion. The pressure wasn't external; it stemmed from my internal critic, the voice of self-doubt that whispered insidious lies of inadequacy. Mr. Evans helped me reframe my inner dialogue, replacing negative self-talk with affirmations of my abilities and resilience. He encouraged me to focus on the process, not the outcome, to celebrate every minor victory, every step forward, regardless of the final score.

The visualization exercises were beneficial. I spent hours picturing myself in the arena, feeling Comet's powerful strides beneath me, hearing the hushed anticipation of the crowd, executing each movement with precision and grace. I visualized perfect performances and potential setbacks, learning to expect and adapt to unexpected challenges. This mental preparation became as crucial as the physical training, allowing me to approach the final round with a newfound calm and control.

Beyond the technical and mental adjustments, I had to refine my communication with Comet. He, too, was sensing the heightened tension. His usually playful demeanor had become more serious, his movements reflecting my anxiety. I groomed extra for him, whispering words of encouragement and reassurance, forging a more profound connection built on mutual trust and understanding. Our usual training sessions developed into silent conversations built on shared intention and mutual respect.

I realized that my connection with Comet wasn't about physical control, but a symbiotic relationship based on mutual understanding and trust. He was my partner, not a tool, and our performance depended on our ability to communicate effectively, to expect each other's needs and respond accordingly. I started paying closer attention to his subtle cues, adjusting my aids in response to even the slightest shifts in his energy or mood. This enhanced communication helped us move as one, our movements seamlessly intertwined, creating a harmonious performance that transcended individual skill.

While initially unsettling, Karen's overt intimidation strategy also provided valuable insight. Her theatrics, her calculated displays of confidence, revealed her vulnerabilities—a deep-seated need for validation, a fear of failure concealed beneath a façade of arrogance. Understanding her tactics allowed me to detach from their emotional impact. I acknowledged her skill, but refused to let her actions dictate my emotional state. I shifted my focus inward, concentrating on my journey, process, and connection with Comet.

The support system around me also transformed. My parents, while still burdened by their expectations, understood the importance of emotional support over constant pressure. They softened their language, replacing critical comments with encouragement and faith in my abilities. They learned to celebrate my efforts, rather than solely focusing on the outcomes, which fostered an environment of unconditional support.

John's steadfast belief in me remained my anchor. Though his understanding lacked technical depth, he provided an emotional perspective that balanced the technical rigor of the competition. Helped me maintain perspective, reminding me of the joy of riding, the bond I shared with Comet, and the intrinsic value of my passion for dressage. He celebrated my journey, not my results. His presence was a constant source of comfort, reassurance, and unconditional love.

The final day arrived with a profound sense of readiness. The electric energy of the arena, once a source of dread, now felt invigorating, a powerful catalyst that fueled my determination. I walked into the warm-up area with a newfound sense of calm confidence, having benefited from weeks of focused training and mental preparation. Sensing my shift in demeanor, the other riders seemed to regard me with a newfound respect.

I focused on my breathing, centering myself at the moment. The visualization exercises came flooding back, each movement sharp in my mind's eye. My connection with Comet felt stronger than ever before. We were a unit, our movements perfectly aligned, our emotions intertwined.

Karen's performance, which preceded mine, was, as expected, flawless. The crowd's roar was deafening, but it didn't affect me. I had transcended the fear of judgment, replaced it with a quiet intensity focused entirely on the performance. This wasn't about winning or losing; it was about executing my plan flawlessly, a testament to my resilience and growth. It was about the connection between Comet and me, a silent language spoken through seamless movement and grace. Entering the arena, I felt a profound sense of peace, a calm acceptance of whatever the outcome might be. The performance was a blur of controlled energy, fluid movements, and perfect harmony between rider and horse. Each transition flowed seamlessly into the following one. The connection with Comet was palpable, a breathtaking display of synchronized movement, a testament to our rigorous training and unwavering bond.

Following our performance, a profound silence descended, thick with the palpable anticipation and electric tension that crackled in the air, leaving the audience breathless in expectation. Every hour of work, every moment of self-doubt, was justified by the rewarding symphony of applause that followed.

Because of the astonishingly high scores from the judges, our performance was incredibly perfect and seamless. However, the actual triumph transcended numerical measures. The victory showed resilience and the deep rider-horse connection, triumphing over self-doubt. My journey of self-discovery culminated in a breathtaking performance, a personal victory. The Grand Prix transcended mere competition; It was a profound testament to the transformative power of perseverance, a narrative of overcoming obstacles, and a celebration of the unwavering bond between a girl and her horse. That personal success mattered more than trophies or praise.

Chapter 18: A Confrontation with Karen

A sharp, brittle voice abruptly shattered the echoing silence after my performance. "Well, well," Karen drawls, her voice dripping with a saccharine sweetness that feels like a venomous insult. She stood near the exit to the arena, her usual entourage of sycophantic friends surrounding her like a protective shield of glitter and self-importance. Her expression, however, lacked its usual theatrical confidence; a flicker of something akin to...fear? Or perhaps it was simply annoyance, masked by practiced nonchalance. Regardless, it was a crack in her carefully constructed façade of invincibility.

I didn't respond immediately. I was still basking in the afterglow of my performance, the lingering euphoria of flawless execution, and the sheer joy of sharing achievement with Comet. Her words, barbed as they were, couldn't pierce the bubble of contentment that surrounded me. But her presence, looming like a storm cloud on the horizon of my triumph, forced me to acknowledge the reality of our rivalry. This wasn't merely a competition; it was a personal clash, a silent war fought on the backs of magnificent creatures.

Karen took a step closer, her high heels clicking sharply on the polished arena floor, a jarring sound that cut through the remaining applause. "Impressive, I'll admit," she conceded, her voice laced with a condescending tone that grated on my nerves. "But luck plays a part. One slip, one wrong move, and the whole thing unravels."

Her words were a calculated jab, aimed at undermining my achievement. She was attempting to diminish the significance of my victory by suggesting it was a matter of chance rather than skill. I had expected this tactic, a familiar dance of psychological warfare. I would not let her bait me into a verbal sparring match. My silence, however, seemed to infuriate her further.

"You're awfully quiet," she continues, her voice rising in volume. Aren't you going to congratulate me? After all, I still placed higher than you in the overall standings." She punctuated her words with a dismissive wave of her hand, a gesture designed to highlight the supposed irrelevance of my achievement.

This time, I responded. "Higher in the overall standings," I repeated, my voice calm but firm. "Yes, that's true. But you haven't accounted for my performance being undeniably cleaner, more precise, and emotionally more resonant. You can't quantify what judges may miss."

Her carefully constructed facade crumbled. The thin veil of polite rivalry shattered, revealing the raw jealousy and insecurity that simmered beneath. Her smile tightened, her eyes narrowing into slits. "Oh, is that so? Perhaps your little 'emotional resonance' is nothing more than dreaming."

"Perhaps," I counter, meeting her gaze with unwavering confidence. "But the judges' scores seem to suggest otherwise."

The words hung in the air, a silent challenge. Spectator whispers momentarily filled the space. Then Karen's carefully controlled composure finally fractured. "You're insufferable," she hisses, her voice dangerously low. The sweetness was gone, replaced by pure venom.

The confrontation escalated quickly. Initially, silent observers, her friends, chided me with their words. They used the same tactics as Karen—subtle digs, condescending smiles, and dismissive remarks. I responded with calmness, a measured tone that seemed to fuel their anger further. My calm demeanor was proving more effective than any fiery retort.

"At least I didn't resort to cheap theatrics," I mumble, my voice loud enough for those within earshot to hear. The remark drew gasps from the crowd and a sharp intake of breath from Karen. That was my moment. I had finally pierced through her carefully constructed armor of confidence. The comment, while Dressage, wasn't a personal attack. It highlighted a fundamental difference in our riding styles, contrasting genuine connection with manufactured showmanship.

Karen's face flushed crimson. She opened her mouth to retort, but a loud cough broke the tension before any words escaped. Mr. Evans, my coach, appeared on the scene, his tall frame looming over Karen and her companions. His presence, quiet yet commanding, immediately shifted the dynamics of the confrontation.

"Karen," he says, his voice firm but measured, "I believe it's time for you to leave." His tone brooked no argument. There was no anger, no accusation; merely a decisive statement of fact.

Karen, visibly deflated, bristled under his gaze. She glared at me one last time, a look filled with a potent mixture of resentment, defeat, and something akin to begrudging respect. Then, with a final, dismissive flick of her wrist, she turned and stalked away, her entourage trailing behind her like disgruntled shadows.

Mr. Evans turned to me, a slight smile playing on his lips. "Well done, Jammie," he says, his voice gentle but laced with pride. "You handled that with remarkable composure."

"She got under my skin," I admitted, feeling the residue of the confrontation still clinging to me. The adrenaline subsided, replaced by a wave of exhaustion and a lingering sense of unease.

"It's natural," Mr. Evans reassures me. Challenges reveal character extremes. But you showed a level of maturity and self-control that is commendable. You didn't let her provoke you into a senseless argument; you responded intelligently and effectively. And that, my dear, is a victory in itself."

His words were a balm to my frayed nerves. The confrontation with Karen, while undeniably unpleasant, had served as a crucible, testing my resilience and sharpening my focus. Dressage, despite its calm appearance, can be fiercely competitive; composure under pressure is vital, matching technical skill. I had learned a valuable lesson—that true strength lay not in athletic prowess, but in emotional intelligence, in the ability to navigate complex interpersonal dynamics with grace and unwavering self-assurance. The quiet satisfaction of knowing that I had confronted my rival tempered the lingering sense of unease, not with anger or bitterness, but with calm, controlled self-confidence.

The tension remained in the air even as I walked back to the stables. Triumph felt short-lived because of intense pressure and looming defeat. Yet, the quiet confidence that had guided me through the confrontation with Karen settled deep within me, a calm strength I knew would serve me well in the challenging days ahead. The Grand Prix exceeded a mere competition; The rivalry with Karen, as intense and uncomfortable as it was, had become an integral part of this journey, forcing me to confront my vulnerabilities and ultimately emerge stronger and more resilient.

Chapter 19: Support from John and Friends

As I returned to the stables, the lingering tension from my clash with Karen clung to me like a second skin. The adrenaline faded, leaving a bone-deep weariness and a gnawing unease. I half-expected Karen to reappear, to launch another verbal assault, but the stables were strangely quiet, the usual bustle muted, almost subdued. The air hummed with a low thrum of anticipation for the upcoming Grand Prix, but overlaid on that was a palpable sense of something else—a quiet tension, a collective holding of breath.

John was the first to find me, sitting alone on a bench near Comet's stall. As I rode, the rhythmic thud of the horse's hooves provided a comforting counterpoint to the turmoil and anxiety that churned within my heart, a steady beat against the chaos. Seated next to me, he rested his hand lightly on my arm. He completely avoided asking questions about Karen. Amid my turbulent and overwhelming emotions, his quiet presence offered a sense of comfort and reassurance, acting as a tranquil refuge from the storm raging within.

"Tough crowd out there," he says, his voice low and understanding. He knew me well enough to understand that my silence spoke volumes. I nodded, unable to find the words to articulate the complex. Emotions churned within me: the lingering adrenaline rush, the exhaustion, the quiet satisfaction of having held my ground, and the underlying fear that still gnawed at the edges of my confidence. The victory felt bittersweet; it was a triumph over Karen and a stark reminder of the fierce competitiveness of the equestrian world and the relentless pressure to succeed.

He squeezed my arm gently. "You did amazing, Jammie. Seriously. I saw your ride. It was flawless." His genuine admiration, unburdened by the competitive pressures of the arena, was a welcome balm.

We sat in comfortable silence for a while, the only sound the soft whinny of Comet from her stall. The horses, these magnificent creatures who had become such a crucial part of my life, seemed to sense my emotional state, offering a quiet empathy that words could not convey. Comet nudged my hand through the bars of her stall, her soft muzzle a comforting weight against my palm. The simple act of stroking her smooth coat was soothing, grounding me in the present moment.

Later that evening, Sarah and Emily, my closest friends, joined us.

They had witnessed the confrontation with Karen and had their own stories to share about the petty rivalries and veiled insults that permeated the atmosphere of the competition. They, too, had experienced the pressure to succeed, the weight of expectation, and the constant undercurrent of unspoken competition. Their support wasn't about congratulating me on my ride; it was about sharing a collective experience, acknowledging the shared struggles and triumphs that shaped their lives as young equestrians.

"That, Karen," Sarah says, shaking her head in disbelief. "She's insufferable. Seriously, how can someone be so completely devoid of grace?"

Emily nodded in agreement. "She's all flash and no substance. You handled her perfectly, Jammie. Honestly, I would have lost it."

Their words were like a warm blanket, wrapping around me, shielding me from the lingering chill of the confrontation. Their presence, their understanding, and their unreserved support provided a safe space to process my emotions, shed the mask of composure I had worn throughout the day, and allow myself to be vulnerable.

John listened patiently as we recounted the day's events, offering insights and sharing perspectives. He knew equestrian life intimately, not from the sidelines, but from years of immersion. He understood the pressure, the sacrifices, and the sheer determination it took to reach this level of competition.

"You know," he says thoughtfully, "Sometimes, winning isn't about the ribbons and the trophies. It's about demonstrating resilience, handling pressure, and maintaining your integrity in adversity." His words resonated deeply, far beyond the immediate context of the competition. They spoke to a larger truth — a fundamental principle that extended beyond the world of equestrian sports—that true strength lies not in technical skill, but in emotional intelligence, in the ability to navigate the complexities of human interaction with grace and unwavering self-confidence.

As we continued to talk, sharing stories and jokes, the tension that had clung to me all day dissipated. Genuine and uninhibited laughter filled the air, a powerful antidote to the negativity that had permeated the earlier confrontation. It reminded me I wasn't alone in this journey, that I had a strong support system to lean on when the pressure mounted, the doubts crept in, and the challenges seemed insurmountable.

In bed that night, the day's events unfurled in my thoughts. The intensity of the competition, the exhilaration of my performance, the confrontation with Karen, the unwavering support of my friends, and John converged into a tapestry of experiences that defined this journey. I realized that the Grand Prix wasn't about winning or losing; it was about growth, self-discovery, and forging bonds that would last a lifetime.

Time flew by in a whirlwind of activity as I frantically prepared for what lay ahead over the next few days. As a significant and daunting challenge, the Grand Prix loomed large, severely testing the limits of my physical and mental endurance and stamina. There was an immense amount of pressure, and the expectations were so high that they were almost unbearable for everyone involved. Despite the chaos and the intense stress that surrounded me, I discovered a haven of peace and comfort in the steadfast support provided by my friends and, in particular, by John. They provided me with a sense of grounding, stability, and refuge during difficult times, acting as anchors in the storms of my life.

John helped me with my routine, offering suggestions and encouragement. He wasn't a boyfriend; he was a supportive teammate, a confidante, and a source of unwavering faith in my abilities. His belief in me, unshaken by my self-doubt, was invaluable. Helped me refine my strategy, focusing on my strengths and mitigating my weaknesses. Helped me strategize, anticipating Karen's moves and preparing for any eventuality.

Sarah and Emily joined me in training sessions, offering encouragement and camaraderie. They pushed me to my limits, reminding me of my capabilities. Their presence lightened the weight of expectation, transforming what could have been a soul-crushing experience into a shared adventure. They distracted me from anxieties about the competition, sharing stories and laughter, lightening the mood, and bolstering my confidence. We spent hours perfecting the choreography, working on transitions, fine-tuning every movement, and they were the best support system a rider could ask for. We practiced our routines under different conditions and scenarios, ensuring I could handle any surprises during the competition.

Their support transcended the physical realm, encompassing a broader, more profound level of help and encouragement. With their help in managing mental pressure, I learned to focus on my strengths, trust my instincts, and believe in myself. I received reassurance and mindset advice to help me succeed, thanks to their listening ear concerning my anxieties. Understanding my burden and the challenge's size, they listened to my worries without criticism.

Knowing they were there constantly reassured me I wasn't alone, that I had a team supporting my every move. Because they believed in me and had unwavering confidence in my abilities, I could approach the Grand Prix with courage and steadfast resolve. I couldn't have succeeded without their support; it was an indispensable element that played a crucial role in my accomplishments. My victory proved my skill and dedication, but also the power of friendship, community, and genuine support. My victory wasn't a solo accomplishment; instead, it resulted from teamwork and collaboration with others.

Chapter 20: Unexpected Setbacks

The morning of the Grand Prix dawned bright and crisp, the air alive with the nervous energy of both competitors and spectators.

But the optimism was short-lived. A sudden, sharp pain shot through Comet's leg as they saddled her. The vet, summoned immediately, confirmed my worst fears: a slight strain in her suspensory ligament. It wasn't a catastrophic injury, but it was enough to throw everything into jeopardy. My carefully laid plans, the weeks of meticulous training, and the unwavering belief in my abilities seemed to crumble in the face of this unexpected setback.

Everything felt disorienting. One minute, I was brimming with controlled confidence, visualizing my flawless performance, the ribbon gleaming around Comet's neck; the next, I faced the terrifying prospect of withdrawing from the competition. The weight of disappointment pressed down on me, heavy and suffocating. This wasn't about the Grand Prix but about years of dedication, countless hours spent perfecting my skills, and the unwavering commitment to my dream. The thought of relinquishing everything, of seeing my hard work vanish, was almost unbearable.

John, the pillar of strength, was by my side, offering calm reassurance amidst the storm of my emotions. He listened patiently as I poured out my frustration, fears, and agonizing self-doubt. He didn't offer empty platitudes or facile reassurances; instead, he acknowledged the validity of my feelings, validating my disappointment without minimizing the gravity of the situation.

"It's okay to feel this way, Jammie," he says, his voice gentle but firm. "It's a tremendous blow, no doubt about it. However, we need to think clearly and rationally. What are our options?"

His words, though simple, were a lifeline. They rescued me from despair, showing me a way forward despite crushing disappointment. We sat together, brainstorming potential solutions and weighing the pros and cons of various scenarios. Could Comet still compete? Should we risk further injury? What would be the consequences of withdrawing? Every option presented its own set of challenges and potential for heartache.

After a thorough examination, the vet offered a glimmer of hope. He suggested a course of treatment—anti-inflammatory medication, rest, and careful monitoring—that might allow Comet to compete, albeit with a changed performance. It was a risky gamble, but further injury seemed less daunting than withdrawal.

The news sent a ripple of anxiety through our support team. Sarah and Emily, ever loyal and supportive, rallied around us, offering practical help and emotional support. They helped me prepare Comet for the changed routine, ensuring she was comfortable and prepared for the competition, despite the setback. They adjusted the choreography, eliminating any movements that might exacerbate her injury, creating a sequence that minimized her leg stress while showcasing Comet's grace and elegance. Their dedication was unwavering and their commitment to our success was absolute.

The pressure was immense, amplified tenfold by the unexpected twist. Every movement, transition, and glance towards Comet's leg was fraught with tension. The fear of causing further harm overshadowed the joy of competing. Every stride and turn was a testament to Comet's resilience, to our collective determination not to give up.

The competition itself was a blur of adrenaline, anxiety, and intense focus. Once a source of exhilaration, the familiar roar of the crowd now felt like a constant threat, a reminder of the high stakes involved. The judge's scrutiny was even more intense, every subtle movement of Comet's leg under observation. Every muscle in my body was tense, every breath carefully controlled.

Despite the strain, the changed routine went surprisingly well. Comet performed beautifully, demonstrating her exceptional training and innate grace, even with the limitations of her injury. Sensing the drama, the crowd reacted with enthusiastic support, their cheers a lifeline in the face of immense pressure.

But the relief was short-lived. During the final canter, Comet stumbled slightly, a barely perceptible falter that sent a wave of panic through me. The pain was clear in her eyes, a stark reminder of the fragile nature of our situation. I brought her to a halt, my heart pounding, the weight of fear pressing down on me again. With grave concern, the vet rushed to the arena to examine Comet. A palpable tension filled the arena; it was as thick as if you could cut it with a knife.

With a gravity that stunned the courtroom, the judges announced a verdict of such devastating impact that it left everyone speechless. A small stumble worsened the athlete's previous injury, forcing his withdrawal from further competition. As I looked into Comet's eyes, I saw the deep disappointment etched on her beautiful face, and tears welled up in my own eyes, not because of the missed opportunity, but because of the pain I saw reflected there. The culmination of weeks of hard work ended in a bitter pill to swallow, an agonizing setback we had to endure.

The withdrawal was a crushing blow, but it brought with it a profound sense of relief. The relief of knowing that I had done all I could, that I hadn't pushed Comet beyond her limits, that my commitment to her well-being was paramount.

Though the outcome wasn't what I had hoped for, the experience strengthened my resolve. It deepened my understanding of the delicate balance between ambition and compassion, between pursuiting excellence and the well-being of my equine partner. The Grand Prix may have ended in disappointment. Still, it taught me a valuable lesson: that ribbons and trophies do not always define genuine victory, but by the unwavering commitment to the journey itself, the lessons learned along the way, and the enduring bond forged with the magnificent creature by my side.

Comet's well-being outweighed everything else. Looking back, the unexpected setbacks revealed both the depth of my love for him and the resilience within me. The Grand Prix, though it ended in disappointment, shaped me more profoundly than any victory ever could. The shared experience of overcoming this obstacle solidified my bond with Comet, Sarah, Emily, and John, proving the importance of teamwork and support in facing adversity. More valuable than any trophy, I learned the importance of resilience, compassion, and the true meaning of partnership.

Chapter 21: A Critical Mistake

Despite the success of the modified routine in helping Comet recover from his injury, I found myself emotionally exhausted from the experience. Although the performance finished, gnawing anxiety and unease overshadowed my relief. The stumble I felt seemed to unveil a deeper, more significant truth or issue than was initially apparent. The rush of performing masked the true extent of the problem, adrenaline obscuring the issue's immense scale.

My heart hammered against my ribs as I waited for the vet's assessment. Deafening quiet reigned. Only quiet whispers and nervous foot shuffling punctuated the arena's silence.

Each second dragged on like an eternity, intensifying my already mounting anxiety. I felt Comet trembling beneath me, her breath quick and shallow. Pain and exhaustion dulled the brightness of her usually sharp, intelligent eyes, reflecting my struggle.

The vet's verdict was a crushing blow, confirming my deepest fears. The stumble had indeed aggravated the injury, making further competition unwise and potentially harmful to Comet. Withdrawal was no longer a possibility; it was a necessity. The wave of disappointment that washed over me was almost unbearable. It wasn't the lost opportunity, the shattered dreams; the guilt gnawed at me, a bitter taste in my mouth. I had made a critical mistake, and the consequences were devastating.

During the final canter, in my desperate attempt to maintain the rhythm and showcase Comet's elegance despite her discomfort, I had inadvertently leaned too heavily on the inside rein, extra pressuring her strained suspensory ligament. Adrenaline, performance pressure: I forgot the vet, the routine changes, Comet's health. My focus on the competition, the judges' scores, and the winning had closed my eyes to the subtle signs of discomfort and Comet's unspoken pleas for me to slow down and ease the pressure.

The tears welled up, blurring my vision. This concerned something other than the Grand Prix. It was about the unspoken communication, the intuitive understanding between us, a bond that had been strained, perhaps even broken, by my reckless ambition.

The weight of my mistake pressed down on me, heavy and suffocating. Previously exciting whispers transformed into accusations. Each sympathetic glance, each murmured word of comfort, was a sharp reminder of my failure, of the disappointment I had caused not only myself but also Comet, my dedicated team, and John.

John's presence was a lifeline in the storm of my emotions. He didn't minimize my guilt or offer hollow platitudes. Instead, he held me close, letting me cry without judgment, letting me express the torrent of self-reproach that threatened to overwhelm me. He understood the gravity of the situation and the depth of my disappointment, validating my feelings without minimizing my responsibility.

"It wasn't intentional, Jammie," he whispers, his voice a soothing balm against my raw emotions. "You were under immense pressure and doing your best for both of you. Self-criticism intensifies under pressure. But it's important to remember that you're not alone in this."

His words were a gentle nudge toward self-forgiveness, a reminder that mistakes are inevitable, especially when dealing with the complexities of high-stakes competition. Helped me process my emotions, reminding me that while my mistake had grave consequences, it didn't diminish my skill or dedication.

Sarah and Emily, my steadfast supporters, were equally understanding. They had witnessed the intense pressure I was under and the unwavering commitment I had shown to Comet throughout the competition, even in the face of her injury. Their empathy was a comfort, and their words of encouragement were a source of strength. They reminded me that while the outcome was disappointing, my dedication and love for Comet were undeniable.

The days following the competition were a blur of veterinary care and quiet reflection. Comet received intensive treatment, her recovery a slow and painstaking process. I spent hours by her side, tending to her needs, whispering reassurances, and feeling the weight of my mistake. The silence in the stables was a stark contrast to the buzz of the competition, but it provided a space for introspection, allowing me to confront the reality of my actions and their consequences.

This experience, however devastating, forced a much-needed recalibration into my understanding of competitive dressage. My relentless focus on winning and meeting the expectations of my family and others had almost blinded me to the most critical aspect: my horse's well-being. The competition, accolades, and ribbons all paled compared to the bond I shared with Comet. My mistake became a harsh yet invaluable lesson. It was a painful awakening, a reminder of the fragile balance between ambition and compassion, between striving for excellence and safeguarding the well-being of my equine partner.

I spent the following weeks rehabilitating Comet, working closely with the vet, and adjusting my training methods. The experience profoundly changed my perspective. I focused on developing a deeper connection with Comet, paying closer attention to her subtle cues and physical and emotional needs. I learned to listen more intently to her body, understand her limitations, and prioritize her well-being above all else.

This wasn't simply about physical rehabilitation; it was also about emotional healing. Rebuilding was necessary for the damaged trust. It required patience, understanding, and an unwavering commitment to prioritizing Comet's comfort and well-being.

I began incorporating more mindful exercises into our training regimen, focusing on relaxation techniques to promote her mental and physical equilibrium. The sessions prioritized collaboration over pushing limits. I revisited the fundamentals of dressage, focusing on clarity, precision, and mutual respect.

Slowly but surely, Comet's recovery progressed. Her leg healed, her gait became smoother, and her energy returned. With each successful training session, my confidence grew, the guilt lifted, and the improvement was incremental. The renewed connection with Comet was a balm to my soul, a testament to the resilience of our bond.

Although challenging, the road to recovery ultimately proved transformative. It forced me to confront my flaws, to acknowledge my mistakes, and to learn from them. It deepened my empathy not only for Comet but also for myself. I understood ambition needed compassion, excellence, and well-being. The Grand Prix might have ended in disappointment. Still, it marked the beginning of a new chapter, one of deeper understanding, renewed purpose, and a profound appreciation for the intricate dance between humans and horses. This newfound wisdom became the foundation for my future success, proving that true victory lies not in winning, but in the journey itself.

Chapter 22: Self-Doubt Returns

The stables, formerly a refuge, now felt like a prison. Comet's steady progress in recovery was a small beacon in the overwhelming darkness of my self-doubt. The Grand Prix, the crushing disappointment, the weight of my mistake swirled within me, a relentless undercurrent threatening to pull me under.

John's unwavering support, Sarah and Emily's gentle encouragement, even Comet's improving condition, couldn't completely quell the gnawing anxiety that settled deep in my gut.

The pressure hadn't lifted; it had simply shifted. Instead of the external pressure of the competition, the judges' scores, and my family's expectations, I now wrestled with the internal pressure of self-criticism. The voice of doubt, once a whisper, had grown into a roaring torrent, echoing my mistakes, magnifying my failures. Each successful training session with Comet was a victory, but it was also a reminder of how close I had come to losing everything.

Sleep became elusive, replaced by restless nights filled with replays of the Grand Prix, each stumble and hesitation replaying in vivid detail. I replayed the moment, analyzing every nuance, every tiny change, searching for a different action that could have altered the outcome. In my dreams, the arena was a battlefield where I struggled against the tide of my self-doubt, while Comet, burdened by my errors, faltered under the pressure.

The days bled into one another, a monotonous cycle of rehabilitation, self-recrimination, and the persistent hum of anxiety. I pushed myself relentlessly, but not in the driven, ambitious way I had before. Now, it felt like a desperate self-justification. I met every tiny improvement in Comet's gait with relief and a bitter self-assessment of my previous carelessness. I was making amends, but the cost felt immense, the shadows of my past mistakes lengthening with every passing day.

My usually sunny disposition dimmed, replaced by a quiet intensity that worried my friends. They tried to rally me, reminding me of my strengths, talent, and bond I shared with Comet. Yet, the shadow of my self-doubt persisted, clinging to me like a persistent mist. My hesitant caution replaced the once-familiar rhythm of our training and the intuitive understanding between Comet and me.

Karen, my rival, remained a constant presence, not a competitor, but a symbol of everything I felt I lacked: unwavering confidence, effortless grace, and an absence of the self-doubt that constantly gnawed at me. I'd see her riding, her movements fluid and precise, and a bitter pang of envy would pierce through my melancholy. It wasn't simple jealousy; it was a profound sense of inadequacy, a realization that perhaps my insecurity wasn't simply a phase but a deep-seated flaw that threatened to derail my aspirations. Watching Karen, I felt a resurgence of the familiar sting of self-criticism, wondering if I had ever truly possessed the unwavering focus. The iron will be required to achieve true greatness in the world of dressage.

While working late in the stables one evening, I stared at Comet, her coat gleaming under the soft light. She nudged my hand with her soft muzzle, and momentarily, the weight of my self-doubt lifted. In her calm presence, in the quiet strength of her gaze, I saw a reflection of my resilience. She had overcome her injury, and I, in my way, was overcoming my self-doubt. The rehabilitation process became a metaphor for my internal struggles. Each small victory, each incremental improvement in Comet's health, mirrored a corresponding increase in my confidence. The physical therapy we undertook together became a mirror for our emotional healing. Slowly, patiently, I rebuilt our bond, strengthening our communication and reaffirming our trust.

The return to competition felt daunting, a re-entry into the arena of my anxieties. The familiar thrill of the competition was now laced with a deep-seated apprehension. A cautious optimism had replaced my confidence, a determination fueled not by blind ambition, but by a deeper understanding of myself and my relationship with Comet. My ride wasn't about awards, ribbons, or fulfilling others' expectations.

The following competitions were far from flawless. There were moments of hesitation, reminders of my past mistakes. But with each performance, I grew stronger, more confident, more resolute. While the judges' scores held some weight, they paled compared to the profound sense of unity I felt with Comet, a calm assurance that washed over me as we moved together in perfect unison, a feeling far more significant than any numerical assessment. Because of the unwavering support and constant encouragement that I received from John, Sarah, and Emily, I could successfully navigate through all the complexities that this new phase presented.

An intense inner struggle locked me in a series of challenging and demanding mental exercises that pushed my limits. I learned to quiet the relentless voice of self-doubt, replacing it with affirmations of my capabilities. I focused on the positive aspects of each performance, celebrating the small victories, acknowledging the progress, and learning from the mistakes.

My perspective shifted. Winning became less about external validation and more about inner peace, about the satisfaction of achieving harmony with my horse. The journey had been arduous, but it was also transformative. The setbacks had honed my skills, sharpened my focus, and deepened my understanding of the intricate relationship between rider and horse. Patience, self-compassion, and forgiveness—especially for myself—became important. The scars of my past mistakes remained, but they were no longer wounds that festered; they were reminders of lessons learned, milestones passed, and a testament to the remarkable resilience of both human and horse. The Grand Prix might have been a turning point, but the actual journey of self-discovery and mastery in dressage was beginning.

Chapter 23: John's Encouragement

The crisp fall air nipped at my cheeks as I walked Comet around the paddock, the rhythmic clinking of her halter countering the rustling leaves. The sun, a weak, watery orb, cast long shadows across the frosted grass, mirroring the lingering shadows in my heart. Even with Comet's steady improvement, a persistent unease lingered, a subtle tremor beneath the surface of my regained composure. The Grand Prix failure continued to haunt me, a recurring nightmare that played on an endless loop in my mind.

John found me there, silhouetted against the fading light. He didn't speak immediately, but he came and stood beside me, his hand resting lightly on Comet's neck. The warmth of his presence was a comforting balm, easing the tension that coiled in my shoulders. Comet, sensing the shift in atmosphere, nuzzled against his hand, her soft breath puffing out a small cloud of mist.

"She's doing beautifully," he says, his voice low and steady, a reassuring anchor in the storm of my anxieties. "Look at her, Jammie. She's strong, she's resilient, and she's ready." His words weren't about Comet; they were a subtle, yet powerful, affirmation of my strength.

I looked at Comet, her coat gleaming softly in the fading light. His words were a mirror reflecting my capacity for resilience. I had underestimated my fortitude, as I had underestimated Comet's. We both faced hardship, emerging stronger.

"It's not about the ribbons, is it?" he asks softly, his eyes searching mine. It centers on connection, partnership, and unity. Remember that." His words struck a chord, resonating with the truth of my feelings. I'd lost sight of that essential truth in the relentless pursuit of perfection, in the crushing weight of expectations.

John treated me to dinner that evening. We didn't discuss dressage directly. Instead, we talked about everything else–school, our friends, our hopes and dreams. With unwavering attention, he patiently listened to my concerns, offering gentle insights and creating a safe space for me to express my doubts and fears with no judgment. There was no attempt on his part to solve my problems or give me false hopes of reassurance; instead, he opted for another strategy. Offering a sanctuary from judgment, he provided a secure space in which I could freely examine and unpack my anxieties, feeling comfortable and safe in my vulnerability. More powerful than any amount of motivational speaking, this simple demonstration of acceptance and steadfast support yielded surprisingly potent results.

The next day, we returned to the stables. The tension had eased, giving way to quiet determination. We started with simple exercises, focusing on the fundamental harmony between rider and horse. John observed closely, offering subtle corrections and gentle guidance, never pushing, always encouraging. He pointed out minor improvements and celebrated the most minor victories. His encouragement wasn't about correcting my mistakes, but about building my confidence and reinforcing my strengths. He saw past the shadows of self-doubt, recognizing the unwavering commitment beneath.

He encouraged me to concentrate on the sheer pleasure of riding, emphasizing the intrinsic beauty and grace that existed within the dance-like connection between myself and Comet. Reflecting on our shared journey, the years of dedicated effort, and the countless hours we invested in perfecting our skills, he helped me to remember and reconnect with the intuitive understanding that has always been a hallmark of our relationship. Through this process, I could rediscover not only the natural fluidity of our movements as a couple, but also the deep harmony that defines our relationship. He reminded me that our connection transcended the pressures of competition and that our bond was a testament to our shared resilience and strength.

Slowly, carefully, we rebuilt the foundation of our partnership. We began with the most fundamental exercises, re-establishing precise cues, subtle weight shifts, and the intricate dance of communication. John watched, offering gentle corrections, insightful observations, and guidance as precise and delicate as a surgeon's touch. He helped me refine my position and improve my balance, reminding me to listen to Comet, feel her subtle responses, and understand the nuances of her body language.

His insights were more than technical corrections. They were subtle acts of encouragement, affirmations of my abilities, and reminders of my innate talent. He challenged me to trust my instincts, my training, and my bond with Comet. He reminded me that the mistakes I'd made were not a reflection of my capabilities, but simply a testament to the inherent challenges of competition.

Each training session was a testament to his belief in me, a manifestation of his unwavering support. Although he wasn't my boyfriend, he served as my mentor, confidant, and the unwavering rock upon which I leaned for support and guidance. Recognizing the pressures I faced and the crippling self-doubt that threatened to engulf me, he showed empathy and understanding. He recognized the heavy weight of my family's legacy and the expectations pressing down on me. Seeing past my self-doubt and anxieties, he recognized and acknowledged the potent strength, impressive talent, and unyielding determination that I truly possessed.

As the weeks passed, a subtle shift occurred. The crippling fear receded, replaced by a quiet confidence, a growing sense of self-belief. I listened to Comet more intently, feeling the subtle nuances of her movements and responding to her with greater sensitivity. Our partnership became more fluid and harmonious; our movements were a seamless blend of strength and grace. John's encouragement had not merely healed a wound, and it had fostered a transformation, a profound evolution in our relationship, both with each other and with our shared passion for dressage.

One crisp morning, as the sun painted the sky with hues of gold and rose, we rode together in the arena. Comet moved with a newfound grace and power, her movements fluid and precise, her responses to my cues instantaneous and intuitive. I rode with a newfound confidence, a quiet certainty, my body moving in harmony with hers. It wasn't about the technical perfection of our movements; it was about the seamless connection—the unspoken understanding that flowed between us, a partnership forged in adversity, strengthened by mutual support, and fueled by an unwavering belief.

The return to competition wasn't a triumphant comeback, marked by effortless victories. There were stumbles, moments of hesitation, reminders of my past anxieties. But with each performance, my confidence grew stronger and more resilient. The scores of the judges held less weight than the feeling of oneness with Comet, the comforting assurance that settled upon me as we moved, a dance of shared strength and grace.

John consistently supported us from the stands. His unwavering support was a tangible force, a quiet affirmation of belief. His encouragement wasn't words of praise; it was a silent language of trust, a constant reassurance that he was there, standing beside me, through every triumph and every stumble. He understood that the journey of self-discovery, of mastering the intricacies of dressage, was a path we traveled together.

And so, with John's patient encouragement, a new chapter began. Self-doubt loomed large at the Grand Prix, yet the race also showcased the profound impact of love, support, and a strong partnership's healing power. The scars of the past remained, but they were now badges of honor, reminders of the lessons learned, the challenges overcome, a testament to our shared resilience, a profound affirmation of our bond.

Chapter 24: A Chance Encounter

The quiet confidence I'd painstakingly rebuilt cracked under the pressure of the upcoming regional competition. Doubt, that insidious serpent, had slithered back into my thoughts, whispering insidious lies about my abilities, my worth. Even with John's unwavering support, a knot of anxiety tightened in my stomach.

Comet sensed my unease. Her usually calm demeanor subtly shifted, a subtle tension replacing her usual relaxed gait. We were in the warm-up arena, the air thick with the nervous energy of other competitors, the scent of horses and sweat hanging heavy in the air.

I meticulously went through our routine, focusing on each movement and transition and trying to shut out the whispers of doubt. Increased concentration heightened the tension. My movements became stiff, my cues hesitant, and Comet mirrored my uncertainty. She wasn't responding with her usual precision, her movements slightly hesitant, almost as if she sensed my inner turmoil.

Then I saw her—a woman with silver-streaked hair pulled back in a neat bun, her eyes crinkling at the corners as she watched me. She wore simple, practical riding clothes, not the flashy attire of the other competitors. There was an air of quiet authority about her, a stillness that belied the intensity of her gaze.

She approached me after my less-than-stellar warm-up; her smile was gentle but firm. "You're Jammie, aren't you?" she asks, her voice calm and reassuring. "I'm Eleanor Vance. I've been watching you ride."

My initial reaction was to shrink back, apologize for my performance, and explain my fumbled movements. But something in her calm demeanor stopped me. There was no judgment in her eyes, only a keen observation, a quiet understanding.

"I've seen many riders," she continues, as if reading my thoughts, "especially inexperienced riders whose anxieties overshadow their talent. I've been there myself."

She talked, not about the technical aspects of dressage, but about the mental game, the importance of inner peace, and the subtle connection between mind and body. She spoke of managing expectations, embracing imperfections, and finding joy in the dance rather than the relentless pursuit of perfection. Her words were like a balm to my frayed nerves, a gentle hand guiding me through the turbulent waters of self-doubt.

Eleanor didn't offer empty reassurances or simplistic solutions.

Instead, she shared anecdotes from her career, including triumphs and failures, as well as moments of doubt and self-discovery. She described the intense pressure of high-stakes competitions, the crushing weight of expectations, the crippling fear of failure. It was as if she understood the essence of my struggle, the deep-seated insecurities that threatened to undermine my potential.

In her remarks, she highlighted the crucial need for riders to find a harmonious balance between competitive success and the development of a deep, meaningful connection with their equine partners, a connection that transcends the pressures of the show ring. Emphasizing the crucial role of patience, she highlighted the necessity of scrutinizing subtle cues from the horse, attentively listening to its quiet signals, thoroughly understanding its needs, and consistently respecting its physical and emotional boundaries. She emphasized the significance of recalling the reasons behind our passion for riding, urging us to reignite the joy and pure delight inherent in the unique partnership between horse and rider, a partnership that elevates riding to the level of a graceful dance and a refined art form, the very essence of equestrianism.

Her advice extended beyond the realm of dressage. She spoke about life's inevitable challenges, the importance of resilience, learning from setbacks, and using adversity as fuel for growth. She shared insights into coping with stress, managing expectations, and maintaining a positive attitude. It wasn't about winning ribbons; it was about personal growth, self-discovery, and pursuing excellence for its own sake.

We talked for over an hour, the sun setting, casting long shadows across the arena. As she spoke, the tension in my shoulders gradually eased, replaced by a quiet calmness, a newfound sense of perspective. She didn't provide magical solutions or quick fixes, but she helped me challenge my limiting beliefs, and rediscover my passion.

When we finally parted ways, I felt a profound sense of gratitude. Eleanor hadn't offered technical advice, but a much-needed dose of wisdom, empathy, and support. Her words resonated deep within me, a soothing balm to my anxious heart, a gentle guide leading me out of the darkness of self-doubt.

I returned to the warm-up arena, feeling lighter, less burdened by self-doubt. I re-mounted Comet, and this time, there was a tangible difference. My movements were more fluid and confident, my cues clearer and more precise. Comet responded instantly; her movements reflected my newfound serenity, and her gait was fluid and graceful. We danced together, not going through the motions, but truly connecting and sharing the pure joy of our partnership.

The subsequent performance wasn't perfect, but it was undoubtedly better — a testament to Eleanor's wisdom — and I had a newfound inner peace. I didn't win, but I rode with confidence I hadn't experienced in months, a confidence that stemmed not from external validation but from an inner strength I had rediscovered.

I shared my encounter with John that evening, recounting Eleanor's words, insights, and inspiring stories. He listened patiently, his eyes filled with admiration and understanding. He knew how much I struggled with self-doubt, how easily I could get lost in the vortex of my anxieties. Eleanor's words mirrored the support he had constantly given me, reinforcing his messages of encouragement and belief.

In the following weeks, Eleanor and I continued to exchange emails, sharing our thoughts and experiences. She became a mentor, a source of inspiration, a trusted confidante. She was the person who quietly encouraged growth without imposing expectations and instilled inner strength that extended far beyond the dressage world. Our chance meeting during warm-ups unexpectedly blossomed. This connection transformed my riding and overall perspective on life, competition, and pursuiting excellence. It was a turning point, not for my riding, but for my life. The Grand Prix had been a crucible, but Eleanor's wisdom and John's unwavering support helped forge me into something more substantial, resilient, and confident, both in the saddle and beyond.

Chapter 25: Regaining Confidence

The regional competition loomed as a stark reminder of the expectations weighing on my shoulders. But something had shifted. Eleanor's words, like tiny seeds of wisdom, had taken root within me, quietly nurturing a burgeoning confidence. The familiar nervousness remained; however, it felt altered. It wasn't the all-consuming terror that had previously paralyzed me. It was a manageable tension, a healthy awareness, rather than a crippling fear.

I started by focusing on Comet. We spent hours together, not practicing our routine, but rediscovering the joy of our partnership. We'd go on leisurely hacks through the woods bordering the stables, letting Comet dictate the pace, feeling the rhythm of her strides beneath me. I listened to her subtle cues — her weight shifts, her soft sighs — and understood her mood and needs. It was a meditative exercise, a way to reconnect with the essence of our bond, stripped bare of the pressure of competition. I started noticing things I'd missed before—the way she'd playfully nudge my hand with her nose, the soft flick of her tail when she was content, the subtle shift in her ears when she was listening intently.

Our training sessions took on a new quality. It wasn't about achieving flawless execution, but about improving our communication and connection. I trusted my instincts, feeling Comet's response rather than relying on visual cues. We focused on the minor details, perfecting transitions, refining movements, and honing the grace and precision of our performance. It resembled a collaborative artistic and athletic performance more than work. I felt her responding to my growing confidence; her movements became lighter, more responsive, and more fluid. The hesitation was gone, replaced by a shared understanding, a harmonious flow of movement.

As Eleanor had so eloquently put it, I refocused my attention on mastering the mental game, a concept she had painted so vividly in my mind. Daily mindfulness techniques centered me and freed my mind from distractions. By learning to quiet my inner critic, I've cultivated self-compassion instead of self-doubt. My visualization focused on flawless execution, graceful and precise performance, and achieving our personal best, not victory. This internal change altered how I approached training. The pressure, which had been immense, subsided, offering relief.

John was a constant source of support, reminding me of my strength, my skill, my potential. He'd ride with me, patiently helping me fine-tune my movements, subtly encouraging me to trust my instincts, bolstering my growing self-belief. He listened without judgment, offering words of encouragement and sharing his own experiences with overcoming challenges. Our relationship blossomed during this time, strengthened by our shared passion for horses and our mutual understanding of the trials and tribulations of competitive equestrianism.

The day of the regional competition arrived. The familiar tension was there, but it didn't paralyze me. I'd learned to manage it, harness its energy, and channel it into focused determination. In the warm-up arena, I felt a calm confidence that I'd never experienced before.

Our performance wasn't perfect. There were minor imperfections and the occasional hiccup, but the overall flow was seamless, fluid, and graceful. We moved as one, our movements harmonious, our connection unwavering. I rode with quiet strength, joy, and a profound sense of accomplishment.

The experience mattered more than the outcome. While I didn't win, the judges praised our performance, commenting on our improved precision, our stronger connection, and our effortless grace. More importantly, I had ridden with a confidence I hadn't possessed before—a confidence that wasn't born of arrogance or self-importance but from a deep-seated self-belief, a recognition of my strength, a trust in my abilities, and a quiet contentment in our shared accomplishment.

The satisfaction that followed was immense, far surpassing any thrill of victory. It was a personal triumph, not in the arena, but within myself. I had faced my fears, overcome my doubts, and emerged stronger, more confident, and more resilient. The regional competition had been a significant stepping stone, a testament to my personal growth, not merely a test of equestrian skills.

After the competition, Eleanor reached out to congratulate me. Her words of encouragement and pride meant a great deal to her. She congratulated me on my performance and the journey that led me there, emphasizing that personal growth and self-discovery often transcended the immediate outcome of any competition.

The experience resonated far beyond the equestrian world. I applied the lessons I had learned—the importance of self-belief, the power of mindfulness, and the value of perseverance—to other areas of my life. My academic performance improved, my relationships deepened, and my well-being soared. I began approaching life's challenges with a newfound sense of calm confidence, tackling them with resilience, facing them head-on, and emerging victorious, not in the outcomes. Still, in the growth and self-discovery they engendered.

Looking back, the regional competition wasn't a turning point in my equestrian career, but a turning point in my life. That moment marked my realization that genuine success stems not solely from winning, but from the journey of self-discovery, the cultivation of inner strength, and the unwavering pursuit of personal excellence, both in the saddle and in life. It was the day I stopped competing against others and started competing against myself, striving to be the best version of myself. That triumph surpassed all trophies. As the Grand Prix drew nearer, unwavering determination, unshakeable confidence, and the steadfast support provided by my beloved horse, my boyfriend, and my wise mentor supplanted my initial fear. With all my preparations complete, I felt confident and fully prepared. My strength had increased significantly, surpassing what I had before. To prepare for my journey, I had meticulously arranged all the details and necessities required for air travel.

Chapter 26: Intense Competition

A palpable sense of anticipation hung heavy in the air, causing a crackling energy to fill the space. The usually vibrant and bustling Grand Prix arena was now eerily quiet, possessing an almost reverent stillness that hung heavy in the air. A thick, cloying scent of polished leather and horse sweat permeated the air, combining with the palpable nervous energy that emanated not only from the competitors themselves, but also from their anxious and supportive teams. As I rode, the frantic, hammering rhythm of my heart against my ribs became a wild, internal drumbeat that played along with the steady clip-clop of the horse's hooves on the sandy ground beneath us. Unlike other competitions, this one held a special significance and was not just another event. The moment of truth had arrived, representing the ultimate test of skills and resilience.

Comet, usually a picture of calm composure, was subtly restless. Her breath hitched slightly, her ears swiveled, and her muscles tensed beneath my leg. She sensed my apprehension, mirroring my nervous energy with a subtle shift in her weight. I whispered reassurances, stroking her velvety muzzle, feeling the warmth of her breath on my hand. "It's okay, girl," I murmur, "we've got this." But even as I spoke the words, a flicker of doubt snaked through my carefully constructed composure.

Karen, my formidable rival, was a study in controlled confidence.

Her magnificent animal chestnut mare stood like a statue, radiating an aura of power and poise. Karen seemed untouched by the pervasive tension, her expression serene, almost smug. She gave a curt nod, challenging rather than greeting. The competitive fire in her eyes was undeniable, starkly contrasting the quiet determination burning within me. I focused on Comet, shutting out Karen's presence, arrogance, and apparent attempts to unsettle me.

Early riders delivered impeccable performances, showcasing years of commitment and honed skill in routines that truly reflected their dedication.

The exceptionally high judges' scores set a very demanding standard for the following competitors. The pressure intensified, becoming a physical sensation, a palpable weight that bore down on my chest with increasing force. As each performance flawlessly unfolded, marked by precise execution and graceful movements, the tension in the audience steadily increased, with each subsequent display raising the stakes to even greater heights. A tangible energy of anticipation hung heavy in the arena, vibrating through the stands and echoing off the walls.

I watched, analyzing each rider's performance and noting the subtle nuances and tiny imperfections that separated excellence from perfection. I learned from their strengths, and observed their weaknesses. Time crawled agonizingly. I focused on deep, slow breaths, attempting to control the rising tide of anxiety, keeping my mind clear and my focus sharp. John, perched nervously on the edge of the warm-up arena, offered a reassuring smile, a silent affirmation of his unwavering support. His presence was a calming balm, easing the tension and grounding me.

My turn approached, looming like a dark shadow. The announcer's voice boomed across the arena, announcing our names, Comets and mine. A wave of adrenaline surged through me, momentarily eclipsing my fear. I mounted Comet, feeling her powerful muscles beneath me, her energy shifting, responding to my heightened state. As we entered the arena, the world seemed to fall away, leaving only Comet and me, our shared connection, our singular focus.

The music began, a familiar melody that had guided us through countless rehearsals. The movements flowed, not from conscious effort, but from ingrained muscle memory, from a deep-seated understanding — a harmonious dance between horse and rider. We executed each pirouette, passage, and extended trot with precision and grace, a testament to our unwavering practice. Yet, a subtle tremor in Comet's left hind leg, a momentary hesitation, threatened to disrupt the seamless rhythm of our performance. My heart lurched, fear momentarily eclipsing the carefully cultivated calm.

I reacted instantly, adjusting my position, rebalancing our weight, subtly guiding Comet, and coaxing her back into the flow of our routine. The moment passed, imperceptible to the casual observer, but I felt its impact—a brief, jarring interruption in the otherwise flawless dance. Despite the minor hiccup, we continued, our movements regaining their previous precision, our connection undiminished.

We moved as one, our grace and fluidity unwavering. Years of dedication, plus a quick recovery from a minor setback, resulted in a convincing performance.

The final movement arrived. The extended trot, a showcase of power and elegance, brought the routine to a crescendo. We maintained the rhythm, our movements harmonious, our grace untarnished. Comet's stride lengthened, her energy surging, her muscles flexing, as if celebrating the accomplishment of our routine.

As we finished, a silent wave of relief washed over me, mingling with pride in our performance.

The judges' scores were high, reflecting the seamless fluidity of our routine, despite the brief pause. I dismounted, my legs shaking slightly, but my heart soaring with accomplishment. The results were still pending, but I knew, deep within, that I had given my all. Regardless of the outcome, I had overcome my insecurities, facing the intense pressure with a newfound calmness and self-belief.

The results announcement seemed interminable. The tension in the air was palpable, a heavy blanket smothering any remaining energy. Karen stood stiffly beside me, her expression inscrutable, her posture tense, conveying confidence and apprehension. The announcer's voice, usually booming with enthusiasm, was subdued, almost hushed, as it built suspense until the ultimate revelation.

When he finally announced the results, a mixture of emotions flooded me—relief, pride, and disappointment. We hadn't won. Karen had edged us out by a fraction of a point, an almost imperceptible narrow margin. Then I felt neither bitterness nor resentment. I had pushed myself to my limits, surpassing my expectations, and had ridden my best performance to date. A profound sense of fulfillment quickly replaced the disappointment. The trophy meant less than the journey, less than the personal growth, less than the unwavering support of Comet and John.

The evening ended with a shared celebratory dinner with John and Eleanor. Despite not winning, the celebration felt genuine as we celebrated our shared journey. It was a victory of personal growth, resilience, and the strength forged in adversity. With all its challenges and pressure, the Grand Prix had been a transformative experience, pushing me beyond my boundaries, revealing my strength, proving that even when you don't win the competition, you can still find triumph in self-discovery and the unwavering bond with your horse. More importantly, I learned trophies do not measure genuine success, but the courage to strive, overcome, and grow. The true rewards were the journey, lessons, and personal triumphs.

Chapter 27: Jammies Preparation

The hours before my final round blurred into a whirlwind of activity—a carefully orchestrated ballet of grooming, tacking, and mental preparation. Comet, sensing the shift in the atmosphere, stood patiently as I meticulously brushed her coat, my touch gentle yet firm, a silent conversation passing between us. Each stroke was a reassurance, a promise of our shared journey, a testament to our unwavering bond. Her coat, usually a rich bay, shone with an almost ethereal luminescence under the bright lights of the stables. I meticulously braided her bangs into an elegant style, a small detail showcasing my attention to detail.

The tack, meticulously cleaned and polished to a mirror sheen, gleamed under the lights. Another silent promise of perfection. They checked and rechecked each piece—saddle, bridle, and reins—ensuring everything was pristine and flawlessly fitted for optimal comfort and control. To avoid saddle chafing, they carefully placed the soft pad for the performance. Making sure Comet was comfortable and secure, I checked and adjusted the girths. Gently, I placed the exquisite bridle on her head. The soft leather yielded to my touch, its supple texture a calming contrast to the growing tension.

My preparation was equally meticulous. My riding attire, usually a source of mild anxiety because of the emphasis on precision, felt strangely reassuring today. The tailored jacket, pristine breeches, and perfectly polished boots were more than clothing; they were a second skin, an extension of my body, allowing for seamless movement and optimal control. I checked my helmet, ensuring it was snug and secure, a vital piece of safety equipment. The perfectly fitted soft yet durable gloves provided sensitivity and grip without restricting movement.

My attention turned from outward concerns to a deep introspection, a profound shift in my mental landscape. With my eyes closed, I focused on taking several slow, deep breaths, hoping to center myself and to calm the frantic, rapid beating of my heart. I pictured our routine, envisioning the seamless flow from one movement to the next, each transition a graceful and powerful step in a harmonious and perfectly executed performance. With a determined effort, I eliminated all traces of self-doubt, instead focusing my thoughts on positive affirmations that fueled my confidence and strengthened my resolve. I wouldn't let fear stop me, and Comet's earlier hind leg tremor was a onetime event. Our goal wasn't victory, but showing skill, precision, and teamwork. The performance highlighted months of dedicated practice, the unbreakable bond between horse and rider, and their unwavering commitment.

The memory of Karen's smug confidence flickered through my mind, but I quickly dismissed it. Her arrogance was a distraction, a potential source of doubt. I focused instead on Comet, on the strength in her muscles, the intelligence in her eyes. She was my partner, my confidante, my unwavering support. We were a team.

I spent the next hour walking Comet around the warm-up arena, executing simple exercises to loosen her up and maintain her suppleness. Each movement was deliberate, each stride precise. I felt the familiar rhythm, the harmonious dance between horse and rider, the unspoken conversation of trust and understanding. The warm-up wasn't about physical preparation; it was about mental preparation — a way to fine-tune our connection, synchronize our movements, and ensure that we were perfectly in sync.

The anticipation mounted, a tangible tension filling the air. I could hear the crowd's murmur, the excited chatter, the nervous whispers of fellow competitors. But I remained focused, my attention riveted on Comet, the subtle nuances of her movement, and the rhythm of her breath. I felt her energy shifting, her anticipation building. We were ready.

The announcer's voice, amplified by the arena's sophisticated sound system, boomed across the vast space. My name, followed by Comet's, echoed through the stadium, sending a surge of adrenaline through my veins. Breathless anticipation preceded the music's start; a timeless pause. The familiar melody filled the arena, transporting us to another realm, a world of grace and elegance, a dance between horse and rider.

This time, there would be no hesitation. The extended trot, the pirouettes, the passage, and each movement flowed flawlessly and seamlessly into the next. I felt Comet's power beneath me, her unwavering response to my slightest cues. We moved as one, a harmonious blend of skill and precision, a testament to our tireless practice. Every muscle memory, every carefully choreographed movement, executed with unwavering precision. This was not a routine; it was a conversation, a testament to our connection, a dance of mutual trust and understanding.

The crescendo of the routine arrived—the final extended trot, a breathtaking display of power and elegance. Comet's stride lengthened, her energy surging, her body flowing with effortless grace. The audience held its breath, captivated by our performance. As we completed the last movement, a wave of relief washed over me, a quiet triumph amid the intense competition.

I dismounted, my legs shaking slightly, but my heart swelling with pride. Waiting for the judges' scores was agonizing, and the silence amplified the tension. I saw John's reassuring smile from the sidelines, a beacon of support amidst the uncertainty. Then came the announcement. The score was high, a testament to our performance, reflecting our dedication and bond.

Despite delayed overall results, profound fulfillment emerged. Then, the outcome mattered less. I had faced my fears, overcome my doubts, and delivered a performance that reflected my skill, courage, and resilience. The genuine victory lay not in the placement but in the journey, the growth, and the unwavering bond I shared with my horse. The Grand Prix was a personal triumph, a testament to the power of perseverance, dedication, and the steadfast spirit of an inexperienced rider and her loyal horse. That night, whether we won or lost, I knew I had already won the most significant battle within myself.

Chapter 28: Karen's Performance

The hushed anticipation in the arena was almost palpable as Karen entered. Her presence radiating an aura of practiced confidence that sent a shiver down my spine. She sat tall and straight in the saddle, her posture impeccable, starkly contrasting with the nervous energy that still thrummed beneath my skin. Her horse, a magnificent black stallion named Midnight, mirrored her composure, his powerful physique rippling with barely contained energy. The air crackled with expectation. This wasn't another round; this was the last performance, the culmination of months of intense training and the ultimate test of skill and nerve. Karen commanded attention.

The music began, a powerful and dramatic piece that perfectly complemented Midnight's imposing presence. Karen moved with a precision that was both breathtaking and unnerving. Each movement was a flawless, seamless transition, a testament to years of dedicated training and an innate understanding of her mount. Midnight responded to her every cue with effortless grace, his powerful strides echoing a symphony of controlled energy through the arena. The extended trots were breathtaking, his legs stretching out in a powerful, fluid motion, his body a picture of effortless elegance. The piaffe was exquisite, a mesmerizing display of controlled power and rhythmic precision. Although each movement appeared effortless, he carefully calculated and meticulously executed each one.

I watched, mesmerized, as Karen navigated Midnight through a series of intricate movements, each one demanding both precision and strength. The pirouettes were breathtaking, a whirlwind of controlled motion, executed with a simply astonishing precision. The passage, a showcase of collected energy and suppleness, was similarly stunning, the horse's gait flowing with an almost ethereal grace. Refinement in even the simplest gait transitions showed mastery born from extensive training and profound dressage understanding. It was a performance that transcended mere skill; it was a demonstration of artistry, a testament to the harmonious partnership between horse and rider.

But it wasn't the technical skill that impressed me; it was the way Karen carried herself, with her unwavering confidence and effortless grace. There was no trace of the nervousness that had plagued me earlier; she was entirely in control of herself and her horse. Her movements were fluid and seamless, as if she and Midnight were a single entity, their minds and bodies working in perfect harmony. Serene concentration marked her expression; however, a powerful resolve permeated her demeanor, noticeable from afar.

As the routine progressed, the intricate choreography, seamless transitions, and sheer power and grace of Karen and Midnight's performance captivated me. It was a masterclass in dressage, a flawless exhibition of skill and precision that left the audience breathless. Karen and Midnight executed each movement with almost effortless precision, resulting in seamless and fluid transitions—a testament to years of dedicated training and their deep bond. The extended trot was impressive, Midnight's strides long and powerful, his body moving with an effortless grace that captivated the audience.

Midnight executed the pirouettes with stunning precision, spinning on his hind legs with breathtaking speed and accuracy. The passage, a showcase of controlled energy and suppleness, was equally remarkable, Midnight's gait flowing with an almost ethereal quality. The half-passes were breathtaking, the horse moving sideways with a nearly impossible level of control and precision. Riders rarely displayed such consistent, artistic movement and transitions.

The atmosphere in the arena intensified as the routine neared its end, the tension palpable in the silence between movements.

Karen's face remained impassive, betraying no hint of emotion, but her focus remained unwavering, her attention riveted on Midnight, her every move synchronized with his. There was anticipation, a quiet intensity that built with each passing moment, culminating in a final extended trot that was simply breathtaking.

Midnight stretched out, his stride lengthening into a powerful, fluid motion, his body a picture of effortless grace. The sheer power and elegance of the performance captivated the audience, holding them breathless. As the music swelled to its crescendo, Karen and Midnight executed a final, flawless pirouette, a perfect ending to an ideal performance. A heavy silence descended;

only hushed whispers disturbed it. It was a performance of unparalleled skill and grace, a testament to years of dedication and the unbreakable bond between horse and rider.

Karen dismounted, her face still impassive, but a hint of a smile played on her lips. A thunderous roar of applause erupted, shaking the arena to its very foundations, a sound so powerful it seemed to threaten the structural integrity of the building itself. When the judges finally announced the scores, they matched Karen's performance—an almost perfect score attesting to her skill and dedication. A heavy, silent challenge hung in the air following her performance, a palpable reminder of the exceptionally top bar she had set for the remaining riders to overcome. Her performance forcefully reminded us of our fierce competition and the need to perform brilliantly. It was a performance that would be difficult to forget and impossible to ignore. Despite my admiration for her talent, a wave of apprehension washed over me. The pressure intensified, and I knew my performance would be exceptional, even hoping to match Karen's achievement. The weight of the Grand Prix hung heavy. It was more than a competition; it was a crucible test of our skill and our resilience, courage, and the depth of our connection with our horses. And as I watched Karen leave the arena, bathed in the glow of her triumph, I knew I had to find something within myself to rise to the occasion. My ride seemed a distant echo of what I'd witnessed.

Chapter 29: Jammies' Final Ride

My heart hammered against my ribs, a frantic drumbeat against the hushed anticipation of the arena. The air hung thick with the scent of sawdust and horse sweat, a familiar aroma that usually calmed me, but now only amplified the tremor in my hands. I adjusted my helmet, the cool leather contrasting with the fiery heat rising in my cheeks. Looking down at Comet, my chestnut mare, I felt the familiar comfort of her warm, steady presence. She shifted beneath me, a subtle sigh escaping her nostrils, as if sensing my apprehension. She was my rock, confidante, and partner in this daunting dance of skill and emotion.

The announcer's voice boomed across the arena, calling my name. It felt distant, unreal, as if someone else was preparing for this momentous ride, not me. I took a deep breath, trying to steady my racing pulse, and focused on Comet. Her velvety muzzle nuzzled my shoulder, a silent reassurance that grounded me in the moment. This was it. The final round. Years of training, countless practice hours, and a lifetime of dedication to this sport culminated in this. Everything hinged on this one performance.

The music began—a haunting melody that swelled and ebbed, mirroring the tumultuous emotions churning within me. I'd chosen a piece carefully, one that reflected not only the technical aspects of the routine but also the emotional journey I had undertaken. The opening notes were soft, almost hesitant, mirroring my initial nervousness. But as the music built, so too did my confidence, fueled by Comet's unwavering presence beneath me.

The dancer executed the first movements precisely, honed over years of dedicated practice. The extended walk was fluid and graceful, Comet's gait effortless and rhythmic. But it wasn't technical prowess I aimed to showcase; I wanted to convey the depth of our connection, the unspoken understanding that bound us together. Emotion imbued every movement, a silent conversation between horse and rider, showcasing years of trust and mutual respect.

As the routine progressed, the music shifted, becoming bolder and more demanding. The trot transitioned seamlessly into the canter, Comet responding to my slightest cues with unwavering obedience. The piaffe, a notoriously hard movement, required absolute precision and control. I felt a wave of doubt wash over me as I started the movement, the pressure momentarily stifling my breath. But then, Comet responded, her powerful hindquarters driving her forward in a rhythmic, mesmerizing dance. The collective energy was palpable; a tangible murmur of appreciation replaced the hushed anticipation of the audience.

The passage, a counterpoint to the piaffe's power, showcased suppleness and controlled grace. Comet's gait flowed with an almost ethereal quality, a testament to the hours spent perfecting this delicate dance. I felt a profound connection with her, a sense of oneness that transcended the physical act of riding. It was a silent conversation expressed through movement and music, a testament to our deep bond.

Each movement flowed effortlessly into the next, a seamless transition between power and grace, precision, and fluidity. With meticulous attention to detail, I performed the half-passes; Comet's body bent with effortless precision as we navigated the arena. I could feel the audience's breath held captive, their attention utterly enthralled by the unfolding performance. The pirouettes were breathtaking, a whirlwind of controlled motion, Comet spinning with an accuracy that belied the difficulty of the movement.

The extended trots were my favorite part of the routine, Comet's powerful strides stretching out, her body a picture of effortless grace. I let myself lean into the motion, surrendering to the rhythm of her powerful gait. The speed and flow were breathtaking, pushing us both to the limit, yet within a controlled, artful frame. As she stretched out, her powerful muscles rippled beneath her sleek coat, and her eyes focused on the task ahead. We moved like one entity, bound by a force stronger than words could express.

But this ride wasn't about the technical aspects of dressage. It was also a reflection of my emotional journey. The music, the choreography, and the movements all served as a vehicle for expressing the vulnerability, self-doubt, and ultimate triumph I had experienced throughout this grueling competition.

I let my emotions flow, imbuing each movement with the raw passion and intensity that had fueled my journey.

There were moments of doubt, moments when the pressure almost overwhelmed me. But then, Comet would nuzzle my shoulder, her presence a silent reminder of our shared bond. She was my anchor, grounding me in the moment and providing the stability I needed to navigate the choppy waters of my emotions. It was our dance, our story, our triumph.

As the routine neared its end, I could feel the tension in the arena building. The music swelled, reaching a crescendo of emotional intensity. I knew I had given everything, poured my heart and soul into this final performance. The final extended trot was breathtaking, both powerful and graceful. That final pirouette: a perfect, self-discovering conclusion.

I dismounted, my legs shaking with exhaustion, but my heart soaring with a profound sense of accomplishment. A heavy silence fell, punctuated solely by audience murmurs of approval. The applause finally erupted, a wave of sound washing over me — a testament to my vulnerability and triumph. This wasn't a performance; it was a confession, a release, an outpouring of my soul, both courage and vulnerability intertwined.

The judges announced their scores, which were much higher than I dared to hope for. It wasn't about winning or losing anymore; it was about the journey, the growth, the self-discovery I had undertaken. Standing there, bathed in applause, I realized I had discovered something invaluable: my inner strength to conquer insecurities and the bravery to accept vulnerability. I remembered the ride and the emotions it evoked; the music and applause faded, but the memory remained forever etched in my mind. It was a final ride that celebrated my skill as a rider and the strength of the bond between Comet and me, a testament to our shared journey and the triumph of overcoming self-doubt. My final ride was more than a competition; it was a testament to the power of self-belief and the enduring spirit of the human-animal bond. It was a profoundly personal experience, a moment of self-discovery and fulfillment.

Chapter 30: The Judges' Deliberation

A knife could slice the silence in the judges' room. Three seasoned professionals, their faces impassive masks of experience, sat around a large, polished table. Before them lay the score sheets, a testament to the day's performances, a swirling kaleidoscope of numbers representing years of dedication, sweat, and unwavering passion. The air hung heavy with the unspoken weight of their responsibility to judge fairly the culmination of years of dedication for each rider.

Judge Moreau, a woman known for her unwavering focus and keen eye for detail, tapped a perfectly manicured fingernail against the table, a rhythmic tick-tock accompanying the silent contemplation. She pursed her lips, a slight furrow in her brow hinting at the internal debate raging within. Years of judging Grand Prix competitions had honed her intuition, her ability to discern technical proficiency and the intangible elements: the connection between horse and rider, the artistry, the emotion. She reread Jammie's scores, noting the consistency across the various movements. The technical execution was impeccable, but the emotional depth truly resonated. Jammie's raw honesty shone through despite the flawless movements. The performance lingered, affecting long after its conclusion.

Judge Davies, a man of few words but immense experience, leaned back in his chair, steepling his fingers. He fixed his gaze on the window, the late afternoon sun casting long shadows across the room. His pragmatic approach and focus on the performance's purely technical aspects were his trademarks. He meticulously compared Jammie's scores to Karen, her major competitor.

Karen's performance was flawless, both technically and in terms of precision and control. But did it possess the same soul? The same emotional resonance? He reluctantly nodded. Though perhaps slightly less technically perfect, Jammie's performance had touched something deeper within him. It resonated with a raw and authentic quality.

Judge Petrov, the youngest of the three, nervously adjusted his glasses, his fingers tracing the lines on the score sheets. People knew him for his progressive approach, which valued innovation and creativity alongside technical skill. Jammie's incorporation of her emotional journey into her routine captivated him. The music, the choreography, the subtle nuances in her riding—it was a story, a personal narrative that transcended the mere execution of dressage movements. It was a risk, a gamble, but one that had paid off handsomely.

The silence stretched, punctuated only by the occasional rustle of paper as they revisited notes and reread scores. The weight of their decision pressed down on them, a palpable tension hanging in the air. They weren't judging performances, but dreams, aspirations, and years of dedication. They shaped destinies, celebrating triumphs, and acknowledging failures. The gravity of their task was immense, a responsibility they did not take lightly.

Judge Moreau broke the silence, her voice quiet but firm. "Karen's performance was undeniably flawless," she began, her words carefully chosen, each syllable weighted with meaning. " Technically speaking, it was near-perfect. But Jammie...Jammie's performance was something else entirely."

Judge Davies nodded slowly, his gaze still fixed on the window. "I agree. The technical execution wasn't as flawless, but the emotional depth...the connection between horse and rider...it was extraordinary."

Judge Petrov chimed in, his voice brimming with enthusiasm. "It was a risk, a bold artistic statement. She didn't ride; she told a story. It was innovative, captivating, and deeply moving."

A murmur of agreement passed between them. They had reached a consensus, a shared understanding that transcended the rigid parameters of technical scoring. Jammie's performance, though not without its minor imperfections, had resonated on a deeper level, touching their hearts and minds in a way that Karen's technically superior performance had failed to do. It was a testament to the power of emotional storytelling, the unspoken communication between horse and rider, and the undeniable artistry that could elevate a simple athletic competition to something truly extraordinary.

The deliberation wasn't about numbers; it was about recognizing the intangible qualities that made a performance truly exceptional. It was about acknowledging vulnerability, taking risks, and the courage to bare one's soul before a judging panel and a large audience. And Jammie had done that. She had taken a risk, revealing her vulnerability, anxieties, and fears, transforming them into a performance of breathtaking artistry.

A silent exchange of glances between the judges acknowledged Jammie's performance's profound impact. The judges turned the conversation to specific scores, but they had established the overall sentiment. The powerful emotional resonance, the extraordinary connection between horse and rider, and her courageous vulnerability overshadowed the subtle imperfections in her performance. Its flawless execution, powerful emotions, interesting narrative, and enduring legacy of courage and self-discovery will ensure people remember this performance.

The judges understood that a performance that leaves a lasting impression — a performance that transcends the sport itself and touches the soul — is a performance truly worth remembering. It's a performance that goes far beyond a collection of scores on paper.

Their final scores showed how carefully they had deliberated. Those figures represented something more than just numbers; They recognized her talent, courage, and special bond with Comet. While they'd announce the scores, the real reward was acknowledging her amazing performance. More significant than the competition's outcome were the enduring memories, emotions, and artistic merit of her performance.

As the judges prepared to document their scores formally, anticipation built—not only within the room but also within the arena where Jammie and Comet awaited, their shared fate hanging in the balance. The judges would soon publicly announce their final decision, a culmination of expertise and intuition, shaping the narrative of Jammie's competitive journey and reinforcing the unique magic of the human-animal bond displayed in the arena. The air crackled with the collective breath held by the judges. Everyone eagerly awaited the outcome of this monumental event, a testament to the power and passion of equestrian sports. The scores reflected technical prowess, a profound human connection, a story told through movement and emotion, and a courageous journey of self-discovery.

Chapter 31: The Announcement

The hushed anticipation in the arena was almost tangible. Nervous energy vibrated through the crowd; a collective breath held as the announcer approached the microphone. He cleared his throat; the sound amplified through the speakers, silencing the murmurs and whispers that had filled the space moments before. Held a single sheet of paper, the results of the Grand Prix competition, a document that carried the weight of dreams, hopes, and years of dedication.

He began, his voice rich, "And now, for the moment, we've all been waiting for...the results of the Grand Prix Dressage competition!" The words hung in the air, each syllable heavy with meaning, each pause amplifying the suspense. A collective sigh seemed to escape the crowd, a unified exhalation of nervous energy. Cameras flashed, capturing the expressions of anticipation etched on the faces of the competitors, their families, and the spectators.

He announced the scores of the lesser-known riders first, their achievements acknowledged with polite applause. Each announcement chipped away at the suspense, building the tension to a fever pitch. Jammie, perched on a nearby bench, her heart pounding frantically against her ribs, squeezed John's hand.

His reassuring grip offered a small measure of comfort, but the anxiety was palpable, a living thing that seemed to inhabit the air she breathed. Sensing her unease, Comet nuzzled her shoulder.

The announcer's voice dropped to a lower register, his tone now charged with gravitas. "And in third place..." He paused, the silence stretching, each second feeling like an eternity. The audience gave polite applause to the name he announced. Jammie barely registered it, her entire focus laser-beamed on the upcoming announcement. Her mind raced, replaying the intricate movements of her performance, scrutinizing every nuance, every subtle shift in Comet's gait, and every expression on the judges' faces.

Sounds and movement swirled; Jammie heard the announcement. The judges announced Karen, her rival, as the runner-up. A wave of polite applause washed over the arena, but Jammie felt oddly disconnected, her senses homed in on the singular, looming announcement. Her muscles tightened, her breath catching in her throat. John's hand tightened around hers, his silent support a lifeline in the swirling vortex of her emotions.

The announcer paused, a dramatic beat of silence before he uttered the words that would seal Jammie's fate. "And finally, in first place... with a score of..." he paused again, the suspense unbearable, "... ninety-two-point seven percent... Jammie Thompson and Comet!"

An explosion of sound erupted. The arena was suddenly alive with cheers, applause, and whistles. The sound was deafening, a tidal wave of joy and relief crashing over Jammie. Tears welled in her eyes, blurring the cheering crowd. She felt John's arms around her, his hug tight and comforting, as she buried her face in his shoulder, sobbing uncontrollably.

Overwhelming joy erased pressure, self-doubt, and fear of failure. The victory wasn't about the scores but the journey, the struggles, the growth, and the unwavering support of her family, friends, and John. The victory was the culmination of months of relentless training, early mornings, late nights, and countless hours spent building a bond with Comet, forging a connection that had transcended the simple rider-horse relationship and become something more profound and enduring.

Comet, usually reserved, seemed to sense her joy, nuzzling her hand, whinnying softly, and bowing his head. Jammie reached out, stroking his soft coat, her tears mingling with the sweat on his flanks. Everyone in the arena could see the bond between them, visible in their synchronized movements and shared heartbeat. The cheers continued, a thunderous testament to their achievement. The judges' faces now softened, smiled, and nodded, acknowledging Jammie's performance's profound artistry and emotional depth.

A flurry of activity followed the announcement.

Photographers surged forward, capturing the moment—the joy, the relief, the mutual admiration between Jammie and Comet.

Reporters jostled for position, microphones extended, eager to capture Jammie's reaction. She stood, slightly overwhelmed but composed, accepting congratulations from fellow competitors, coaches, and family members. Despite her loss, Karen offered a genuine smile of congratulation, her competitive spirit overshadowed by a newfound respect for Jammie's emotional depth and courage.

The victory felt surreal. Her dream manifested, a memory forever. As she accepted the trophy, a glittering symbol of her hard work and dedication, she looked out at the cheering crowd, her heart swelling with gratitude and joy. Victory held no importance; The following celebratory dinner was a whirlwind of laughter, congratulations, and shared memories. John was by her side, his presence a constant source of comfort and support. Her parents beamed; years dedication culminated this triumphant moment. Friends and fellow riders shared their congratulations, and their words were sincere. The air was alive with the infectious energy of celebration, a testament to the equestrian community's shared passion and camaraderie.

The day ended with Jammie and Comet enjoying a quiet evening in the stables. Jammie showered Comet with extra treats, a well-deserved reward for his impeccable performance. As Jammie brushed his coat, her fingers tracing the muscles that had carried them both to victory, she realized that the Grand Prix was more than a competition; it was a testament to their bond, a reflection of their shared journey, a celebration of the human-animal connection that had carried them beyond expectations.

The victory wasn't a personal triumph but a symbol of perseverance, self-belief, and the unwavering pursuit of excellence. It reinforced her understanding that genuine success extends beyond mere technical proficiency, encompassing emotional depth, courage, and the strength to overcome self-doubt. It was a victory that would resonate far beyond the arena, shaping her life's journey and inspiring others to pursue their passions with courage and unwavering commitment. The memories of the day, the emotions felt, and the triumph achieved were far more valuable than any trophy or score could ever be.

Above all else, the journey, the personal growth, and the profound connection with her loyal partner, friend, and confidante, Comet, proved the most rewarding. Although the Grand Prix had concluded, winning unleashed a previously unknown confidence and self-belief, fueling her future endeavors for years. A new dream was growing in her heart.

Chapter 32: Jammie's Reaction

The crowd's roar was a physical force, a wave that crashed over Jammie, leaving her breathless and disoriented. The announcer's words, "9 out of 10... Jammie Thompson and Comet!" still echoed in her ears, a surreal symphony of disbelief and overwhelming joy. John's arms were tight around her, a comforting haven amidst the chaos. His warmth seeped into her, grounding her in the present moment. She sobbed, the tears hot and unrestrained, a release of tension she hadn't realized she'd been holding onto for so long.

It wasn't the victory; it was the sheer relief. The crushing weight of expectation, the relentless pressure she'd placed upon herself, the fear of disappointing her family, her friends, and most importantly, she dissolved in the face of this triumphant moment. The months of relentless training, the early mornings spent grooming Comet, the late nights studying dressage manuals, and the sacrifices she'd made coalesced into this breathtaking moment of validation.

Comet, usually stoic and composed, mirrored her emotional explosion. He whinnied softly, nuzzling her hand, his warm breath against her skin a testament to their deep bond. His gentle movements and quiet reassurance spoke volumes. He'd felt her anxiety, her doubt, her fear. Now, he shared her joy, her relief, her triumph. Their connection transcended the simple rider-horse relationship, a partnership built on mutual trust, respect, and unwavering dedication. It was a connection that had carried them both through countless challenges and ultimately led to this extraordinary victory.

The flood of congratulations was overwhelming. Fellow competitors, coaches, family members, friends—they all enveloped her in a sea of warmth and affection. Karen, her fierce rival, approached with a genuine smile, her earlier arrogance replaced by a grudging respect. "You were incredible, Jammie,"

Karen says, her voice sincere. "Comet was magnificent." The compliment felt unexpected, yet profoundly validating. It recognized her skill, artistry, and emotional depth in her performance.

The sheer pride that Jammie's parents felt was evident in the joyful expressions on their faces, a clear testament to their happiness. Their confidence in her never wavered, not even when she was struggling with intense self-doubt and experiencing her lowest points. She found strength and direction in their constant support during the hard times. Overwhelmed with immense joy and relief, tears welled up in their eyes, a visible manifestation of their profound emotions. The warm embraces they shared were a clear and heartfelt demonstration of the profound love and immense pride they felt.

John, her steadfast rock, stood beside her, his presence a constant source of comfort and strength. He hadn't supported her equestrian aspirations, but understood her struggles, vulnerabilities, and insecurities. His love for her transcended the competition, embracing her flaws completely. His unwavering belief in her had been a constant source of inspiration, a silent encouragement pushing her to strive for excellence.

During the celebratory dinner, there was an abundance of laughter, heartfelt congratulations, and the sharing of cherished memories everyone will always remember. The celebratory atmosphere was vibrant and contagious. This event showcased the equestrian community's unity, shared love for horses, and mutual respect, creating a joyful and successful atmosphere. Jammie was deeply grateful and appreciative of those who had shown her unwavering belief, support, and love.

Later that evening, alone in the stables with Comet, Jammie allowed herself to fully absorb the enormity of what she had achieved. The victory felt surreal, a dream she'd dared to dream that'd miraculously become a reality. As she brushed his coat, feeling the soft warmth of his muscles, she realized that the Grand Prix was more than a competition. It was a testament to their bond, a reflection of their shared journey, symbolizing the profound connection between human and animal.

Her win unlocked something within her—a confidence and belief in her abilities that she hadn't known she possessed, and which self-doubt had buried. The victory wasn't about winning; it was about overcoming those inner demons, confronting her fears, and embracing her vulnerabilities. It was about learning to trust herself, believe in her potential, and recognize the power of her connection with Comet.

The Grand Prix trophy, a glittering symbol of her achievement, sat at a nearby table. It was a beautiful object, but it paled compared to the true rewards of her journey. The veritable treasures were the lessons she had learned, the personal growth she had experienced, and the profound connection she shared with Comet. The journey had been challenging, fraught with uncertainty and self-doubt, but it had also been transformative. It had taught her the importance of perseverance, the power of self-belief, and the value of unconditional support.

She stroked Comet's velvety nose. He responded with a soft nuzzle, his eyes intelligent and calm. Looking at him, she saw the reflection of her resilience in his steadfast gaze and felt a surge of gratitude. The victory wasn't hers; it was theirs. It belonged to the quiet moments of training, the shared breaths between them, the unwavering trust that had bound them together.

The victory felt like the culmination of a chapter and the beginning of a new one. The future held new challenges, opportunities, and even greater heights to come. Now, she'd confront them; self-assured, resolute, insightful. The win wasn't a score; it was a transformation. It was the opening of doors she hadn't known existed. Quiet, unwavering self-belief had replaced her fear of failure. The insecurities that had haunted her were now distant echoes, replaced by a calm confidence that pulsed within her, a newfound strength born of perseverance, resilience, and an unbreakable bond with her equine partner.

She spent the next few hours whispering her gratitude into his soft mane. The quiet intimacy of the stable, with its comforting scent of hay and leather, and the rhythmic sounds of Comet's breathing, was her sanctuary. Here, she contemplated her journey, savored her triumph, and planned. The journey had been long, demanding, and emotionally taxing, but it was also gratifying. It had taught her not only about dressage but also about herself, about her inner strength, resilience, and capacity for growth.

Although the Grand Prix had concluded, Jammie's narrative was just beginning. That experience defined both her equestrian career and her life. The confidence that she had gained was not simply about winning, but about the journey of growth and perseverance she had undertaken. Her victory served as a powerful testament to her unwavering perseverance, her immense courage in the face of adversity, and the steadfast support she received from those who believed in her potential, even during moments when she herself doubted her ability to succeed. The future held untold possibilities, but Jammie faced them with a quiet strength she never knew she possessed, a strength forged in the fires of competition, fueled by the unwavering loyalty of her horse, and bolstered by the love and support of her family and friends.

This win was more than a title; it symbolized her triumph over self-doubt, a testament to the human spirit's capacity for growth, and a profound expression of the incredible bond between a girl and her horse. And as she drifted off to sleep that night, the soft sounds of Comet's breathing a gentle lullaby, Jammie knew her journey had only begun. The future held more challenges, opportunities, and heights to achieve. However, she would confront them not with fear, but with a quiet confidence that she had earned through hard work.

Chapter 33: Karen's Reaction

The celebratory atmosphere crackled around Jammie, a vibrant energy buzzing like a thousand excited bees. But amidst the swirling confetti of congratulations and the joyous clamor of well-wishers, Jammie noticed Karen standing a little apart, observing the scene with an intensity that belied her earlier grudgingly offered compliment. Quiet contemplation, intriguing to Jammie, had muted Karen's usual confident arrogance. The victory, so sweet and validating for Jammie, seemed to hold a different resonance for her rival.

Unlike the others, Karen didn't rush to offer another congratulatory hug or boisterous cheer. Instead, she watched Jammie interact with her family and friends, her dark eyes absorbing the scene like a sponge. Her gaze flickered; Jammie sensed not envy, but admiration mixed with something darker, undefinable. A knowing glance revealed a deep awareness of the heavy burden of pressure and expectations.

Later, as the last of the guests departed, and the stables fell quiet, Karen approached Jammie, Comet's gentle snorts providing a calming counterpoint to the still-thrumming energy of the victory. She held a small, exquisitely crafted silver horseshoe in her hand, its intricate details catching the soft light filtering through the stable's open doors.

"I... I wanted to give you this," Karen says, her soft voice contrasting with her usual sharp tone. The offering felt surprisingly intimate, silently acknowledging a shared experience, a tacit understanding that transcended their rivalry.

Jammie accepted the horseshoe, her fingers tracing the delicate curves of the silver. "Thank you," she murmurs, genuinely touched by the gesture. The gift held complexity.

"I... I didn't expect you to win," Karen admitted, her gaze dropping to the stable floor. "I prepared for months. I trained harder than ever before. I thought... I knew... I had to win." The confession hung in the air, heavy with unspoken pressure and the sting of defeat.

Jammie understood. She was aware of the pressure Karen faced, her expectations, and the burden of her family's legacy in the equestrian world. It wasn't dissimilar to the weight Jammie herself had struggled to bear.

"I know," Jammie replies softly, her empathy deepening. "It's... It's a lot to carry."

Karen nodded, a slow, almost painful movement. "My parents...they... they expect so much. They've invested a great deal in me. This wasn't a contest. It was a validation, a proof of my worth." Her words, raw and vulnerable, a side of Karen Jammie that she had never seen before, revealing a profound insecurity beneath the carefully constructed facade of arrogance.

Jammie saw a reflection of herself in Karen's words, a shared experience that transcended their competitive relationship.

"It's okay to feel that pressure," Jammie says, her voice gentle, her words imbued with a newfound understanding and compassion. "But it's not okay to let it define you." She paused, choosing her words carefully. "Winning... It's great, of course. But it's not everything. The real victory... It's in the journey, the effort, and the growth."

Karen's dark eyes met Jammie's; gratitude flickered within them. "I... I didn't see it that way before, "she admitted, a hint of self-awareness in her voice. Outcome obsession eclipsed process, passion, connection.

Jammie smiles with a genuine, compassionate expression. "That's what I learned," she says. "It's not about the ribbons or the trophies. It's about the connection, the dedication, the journey itself." She pointed to Comet, who nuzzled her hand gently. "Comet taught me that. He never judged me for my mistakes. He kept pushing me to be better, work harder, and trust him."

Their conversation continues late into the night, the quiet of the stable offering a sanctuary for vulnerability and shared understanding. During their conversation, they shared intimate details about their families, the pressures they faced in life, and the dreams that filled their minds. In sharing their experiences, they revealed a tapestry woven from threads of triumph and disappointment, each story a testament to the unique bond they held with their horses, from exhilarating wins to heartbreaking losses. People acknowledged the competition, which pushed them both to their limits, as a rivalry. However, the quiet of that night together fostered a new understanding, a recognition of their shared difficulties, and a respect built on mutual vulnerability.

Karen's initial reaction to the results was disappointment, a bitter taste of failure that lingered despite her outwardly congratulatory words. The crushing weight of unmet expectations from her parents and the pressure to uphold the family's reputation left her feeling empty despite her immense talent and years of dedicated training. It was a stark contrast to the joyous exuberance surrounding Jammie's victory.

Meticulous planning, a thorough study of her rival, and relentless horse training characterized her preparation. Success was a relentless pursuit, a burning ambition that consumed her every waking moment and fueled her dreams.

As the immediate pain of the loss lessened, however, a different viewpoint came into focus, altering the initial interpretation of events and offering new insights. As Karen observed Jammie's authentic happiness and the deep, loving bonds she shared with her family and friends, her perspective on the meaning of victory began to shift and develop. It was not about achieving victory; other aspects were more important. The raw, unadulterated joy and relief she witnessed in Jammie's unrestrained victory celebrations stirred something deep within her, a potent mixture of emotions she couldn't quite name.

For the first time, Karen allowed herself to consider the importance of the process, the intrinsic value of the effort itself, and the profound satisfaction that comes from pushing one's limits, regardless of the outcome. She realized that her obsession with winning had blinded her to the true essence of the sport, to the beauty of the art, to the profound connection that could exist between a rider and their horse.

Jammie's victory was a wake-up call, a reminder of the more profound meaning beyond the competition.

The silver horseshoe, a slight gesture, symbolically represented Karen's shift in perspective. It was a silent acknowledgement of her rival's skill and resilience, a grudging admiration for the strength of character, and the unwavering determination that had carried Jammie to victory. It also symbolized Karen's growing self-awareness, as she recognized the need to reevaluate her priorities and redefine her path toward success. The Grand Prix hadn't been a competition, but a catalyst for personal growth — a transformative experience that offered valuable lessons beyond the ribbons and trophies.

In the quiet solitude of her stable, Karen reflected on the events of the competition, replaying the moments in her mind, analyzing her performance, and acknowledging her shortcomings.

The defeat was an opportunity for growth, a chance to refine her skills, strengthen her connection with her horse, and rediscover her genuine love for the sport that had once been so clear. The next competition wouldn't be another chance to win; it would be a chance to prove something to herself, a testament to her resilience, unwavering dedication, and newfound appreciation for the journey.

The rivalry between Jammie and Karen had been fierce, and sometimes even bitter. But a quiet understanding had blossomed in the aftermath of the Grand Prix. Family pressures, high expectations, and the pursuit of excellence molded them. Their paths had intertwined, pushing each other to their limits, forcing them to confront their deepest insecurities and vulnerabilities. Ultimately, competition fostered understanding, respect resulting from shared experience and mutual appreciation for equestrian sports' depth. The Grand Prix had been more than a competition; it had been a crucible, refining their characters, shaping their aspirations, and ultimately bringing them closer together.

Chapter 34: Friends and Family's Support

The celebratory dinner following the Grand Prix was a whirlwind of laughter, hugs, and excited chatter. Still buzzing from the adrenaline of her victory, a sea of familiar faces—her family, her friends, and even a few of her fellow competitors who'd offered surprisingly genuine congratulations surrounded Jammie. Her parents, usually reserved in their displays of affection, beamed with uncontainable pride, their eyes shining with a mixture of joy and relief. Her mother, usually so meticulously composed, even shed a happy tear, clutching Jammie's hand tightly.

"I knew you could do it, sweetheart," her father says, his voice thick with emotion. "All those hours of practice, all that dedication... it paid off," her father says, his words focusing not on the victory, but on her effort.

Her younger brother, Tom, bounced on the balls of his feet, his eyes wide with admiration. "You were amazing, Jammie! Comet was incredible too!" He peppered her with excited questions about the performance, mimicking her movements with a playful exaggeration that made her laugh. His enthusiasm was infectious, a reminder of the simple, unadulterated joy at the heart of her passion for horses.

The celebratory mood swept up even her grandmother, who usually preferred the quiet solitude of her garden. She gave Jammie a delicately embroidered handkerchief, a cherished family heirloom passed down through generations of equestrian enthusiasts. "Always remember this day, my dear," she whispers, her voice raspy but filled with affection. "Remember the feeling, the triumph, the sheer joy of it all." The gift wasn't a piece of fabric but a symbol of her family's unwavering support and shared history with the sport.

Beyond her family, the outpouring of support from her friends was equally heartwarming. John, her boyfriend, stood proudly by her side throughout the evening, his eyes sparkling with affection and admiration. He wasn't a horse person, not in the same way she was. Still, he understood her passion, celebrated her triumphs, and offered unwavering support during her moments of doubt and insecurity. He brought her a bouquet of her favorite wildflowers, a simple gesture that spoke volumes about his thoughtful nature and deep affection for her.

Her best friend, Sarah, a fellow equestrian who'd been her confidante throughout the rigorous training process, squeezed her hand tightly. "I told you could do it!" Sarah exclaims, her voice filled with genuine pride. They shared a knowing look, a silent acknowledgment of the highs and lows they'd navigated together, the long hours spent practicing, the shared anxieties, and the mutual support that'd helped them reach their full potential.

Sarah's presence was a constant source of comfort and strength, a reminder that Jammie wasn't alone in her journey. She understood the unique challenges of balancing the demands of competitive riding with the complexities of teenage life.

The support extended beyond her immediate circle. Other riders, even some who'd been her competitors, approached her with genuine congratulations, their words heartfelt. There was a shared understanding, a silent acknowledgement of the dedication, discipline, and unwavering commitment required to reach the level of competition they all aspired to. It was a camaraderie forged in the fires of intense rivalry, but tempered by a mutual respect for the skill, passion, and unwavering dedication required in their shared pursuit of excellence. The friendships she'd built within the equestrian community extended far beyond the ribbons and trophies. They were bonds built on shared experiences, mutual respect, and a deep love for the sport.

Even the stable hands, who often worked long hours in relative obscurity, offered their heartfelt congratulations. They knew the countless hours Jammie had spent with Comet, the early morning practices, the late-night grooming sessions, and the dedication that went far beyond the hours of formal training. Their unassuming appreciation was deeply touching. It was a reminder that her success was a testament to the collective effort, the shared dedication, and the unwavering support of everyone who'd played a role in her journey.

As the evening drew close and the celebratory atmosphere faded, Jammie sat quietly in her stable, Comet dozing peacefully beside her. The echoes of laughter and congratulations still lingered, but a profound calm settled over her. The victory wasn't a personal triumph; it was a shared experience and a testament to the unwavering support of her family, friends, and the entire equestrian community. The victory had affirmed her skill, her dedication. Still, it had also reaffirmed the importance of relationships, the profound impact of human connection, and the essential role of support in pursuing and achieving one's dreams. Ribbons and trophies symbolized her success, but the enduring victory was the warmth of her relationships.

Interviews, photo shoots, and media appearances blurred together in the following days. The victory had propelled Jammie into the spotlight, and suddenly she navigated the unfamiliar world of fame and recognition. While the attention was initially exciting and validating, it also presented a new set of challenges—managing expectations, navigating the pressure of public scrutiny, and balancing the demands of her newfound celebrity with her commitments to training and personal relationships.

Throughout this whirlwind, however, the unwavering support of her loved ones remained her anchor. Her family shielded her from the more intrusive aspects of the media, helping her maintain perspective and grounding amidst the chaos. Understanding her pressures, her friends provided a much-needed escape, offering laughter and distraction when she needed it most. John, ever supportive, helped her navigate the complexities of her new reality, ensuring she kept her feet firmly on the ground. Their unwavering love and support proved to be her greatest strength, helping her cope with the pressures of fame and use her newfound influence to promote the sport and inspire other young equestrians.

Her success became a catalyst for change within her family. The celebration following her victory had brought them closer together, fostering a stronger sense of unity and understanding. Her always supportive parents showed affection more openly, valuing the importance of emotional expression alongside their previously pragmatic approach to her training. The shared experience of celebrating her success created a deeper bond within the family, forging a stronger sense of shared purpose and mutual respect.

Jammie also attempted to nurture her friendships and relationships, ensuring that her newfound success didn't overshadow the importance of her connections. She took time out of her busy schedule to spend quality time with her friends and family, realizing that her relationships were as crucial to her well-being as her riding. The support she received during the Grand Prix wasn't a onetime event; it was an ongoing source of strength and motivation to guide her throughout her equestrian career.

Ultimately, Jammie's victory at the Grand Prix served as a poignant reminder of the profound importance of human connection. It was a testament to the power of shared experiences, mutual support, and the unwavering love of friends and family. The ribbons and trophies were tangible symbols of success, but the bonds she had forged through her journey proved an even more valuable prize. The victory wasn't solely hers; it belonged to everyone who had played a part in her journey. It was a collective triumph born out of dedication, perseverance, and the unwavering strength of human connection. Success stemmed from supportive relationships, not achievements.

Chapter 35: Reflection on the Experience

The quiet hum of the refrigerator was the only sound in the otherwise silent kitchen as Jammie stared out the window, the pre-dawn light painting the sky in shades of soft pink and lavender. The Grand Prix felt like a lifetime ago, a whirlwind of adrenaline, tension, and triumphant exhilaration. Now, silence followed the applause; she reflected on her achievements and personal development.

It wasn't the victory itself, the gleaming trophy sitting proudly on the mantelpiece, or even the cascade of congratulatory messages that had flooded her inbox. It was something more profound that went beyond the ribbons and accolades. The Grand Prix had been a crucible, forging her into a stronger, more confident rider, but more importantly, a more self-assured young woman.

Before the competition, self-doubt, a crippling insecurity that stemmed from the weight of her family's equestrian legacy, had plagued her. Living up to her ancestors' legacy felt overwhelmingly burdensome. She'd almost let the pressure paralyze her, allowing fear dictating her actions instead of her talent. The memory of those agonizing moments of doubt still lingered, a stark reminder of how close she'd come to letting fear win.

But the Grand Prix had changed that. The competition's challenge and sheer intensity forced her to confront her insecurities head-on. Once a debilitating force, the pressure had become a catalyst for growth. She'd faced the daunting task not only with skill but with a newfound determination, a fierce resolve that surprised even herself. Her precise movements, perfectly synchronized with Comet, showcased dedication, hard work, and newfound confidence.

The memory of Comet's powerful strides, the rhythmic beat of his hooves against the arena sand, and the way he responded to her every subtle cue was a testament to the unspoken language they'd developed — a language forged in countless hours of training and mutual trust. It wasn't a horse and rider; it was a partnership, a bond of mutual respect and understanding, and that bond had been the key to unlocking her potential.

She remembered the almost palpable tension in the arena, the hushed expectancy of the crowd, the focused gaze of the judges. The weight of expectation had been immense, but somehow, she'd risen to the occasion, her nerves transforming into concentrated energy. She executed every movement, every pirouette, and every extended trot with precision and grace.

As she reflected on her performance, she realized that the technical aspects of her riding weren't the most crucial factors determining her success. With a surge of inner confidence, her long-held self-doubt evaporated, leaving her feeling empowered and self-assured. Her riding skills alone did not determine her victory. Through great strength and perseverance, she could finally overcome the many personal struggles and challenges that had plagued her for so long.

In the chaotic and exciting aftermath of the Grand Prix, a truly remarkable and unexpected revelation had unfolded. Numerous interviews, countless photo shoots, and a never-ending stream of congratulations completely overwhelmed and thrilled me. What was once a source of intense anxiety, the attention she received, transformed into a powerful platform from which she could enthusiastically share her passions and inspire countless others. The event allowed for networking with other young riders, provided a platform to share her personal narrative of growth and achievement, and served as a powerful reminder that extraordinary results are attainable through the combination of diligent work, unwavering dedication, and an unwavering belief in oneself.

However, amidst the media frenzy, the constant stream of social media notifications and interview requests, she'd consciously chosen to nurture her personal relationships. She'd learned a valuable lesson about the importance of balance, the need to prioritize her equestrian ambitions, and the bonds that sustained her.

John's unwavering support throughout the competition and its aftermath had been invaluable. His love was a steadfast anchor in the storm of her newfound fame, helping her maintain perspective and stay grounded amidst the chaos. He celebrated her victories without losing sight of the real Jammie, the girl beneath the media spotlight.

Her friendship with Sarah remained as strong as ever, a testament to the resilience of their bond. Their shared journey had created a unique understanding, a silent communication that transcended words. Sarah's empathy and understanding had been invaluable during the challenging times, and their celebrations were even more meaningful for their shared history.

Even her relationship with her family had undergone significant changes. The shared pride and joy in her victory had brought them closer together, bridging the emotional distance that had sometimes existed between them. Her parents' newfound openness in expressing their love and support was a welcome change, a testament to the transforming power of shared success and the importance of familial connection.

The Grand Prix had not only showcased her equestrian talent, but had illuminated the essence of her character. It revealed her strength, resilience, unwavering commitment to her passion, and the profound importance of self-belief. The journey was about discovering oneself, proving the strength of perseverance, and highlighting that genuine victories stem from conquering inner challenges rather than external accomplishments.

Beyond the beautiful trophies and elegant ribbons, her real prize was a newfound self-assurance. The real victory was knowing she had risen to the challenge as a rider and young woman, fully formed and fiercely independent. The journey had changed her; she was stronger, more confident, and fully aware of her unwavering support system in her family, friends, and the incredible bond she shared with Comet. The Grand Prix was a chapter closed, but her life story, rich with challenges and triumphs, continued.

Chapter 36: Life After the Grand Prix

The weeks following the Grand Prix were a blur of activity, a whirlwind that left Jammie breathless but exhilarated. The media attention was intense—interviews, photo shoots, and magazine articles—a constant stream of requests that initially overwhelmed her. Flashing cameras and probing questions thrust her into a new world, a far cry from the quiet solitude of the stables she cherished. The pressure to maintain a flawless public image was immense, a burden that occasionally weighed heavily on her. She carefully crafted her responses, choosing her words precisely, aware that every statement and gesture was being scrutinized.

Yet, amidst the chaos, profound satisfaction lingered. The recognition and accolades were gratifying, a testament to her hard work and dedication. But more importantly, they validated her self-worth, confirming that her years of relentless training and unwavering commitment to her craft had paid off. The victory wasn't about winning; it was about proving to herself foremost that she could achieve her dreams.

She received many congratulatory messages, emails, and social media posts from around the world. Her own had inspired inexperienced riders, seasoned professionals, and even strangers reached out to express their admiration and support. This experience was humbling and ignited a desire to use her newfound platform to inspire others. She realized that her journey, struggles, and triumphs could resonate with many, offering a message of hope and perseverance.

One particular email stood out from a young girl named Emily who lived in a small town in rural Ohio. Emily had been battling self-doubt, struggling with her passion for dressage, and feeling the weight of expectation from her family and community. Jammie's story, her journey of overcoming adversity, had given Emily renewed hope. Reading Emily's words, Jammie felt a profound sense of responsibility, a desire to share her experiences and encourage others to pursue their passions, regardless of the obstacles they faced. She wrote a blog, sharing her experiences, offering advice, and connecting with inexperienced riders worldwide.

The blog became a platform for her to connect with her audience on a more personal level. She shared her training routines, discussed her struggles with self-doubt, and discussed the importance of mental resilience. She answered questions candidly, sharing her experiences with both triumphs and setbacks. The connection with her readers was immediately and deeply satisfying. She felt a sense of community, a shared bond with others who understood the unique challenges and joys of the equestrian world.

Even outside of the virtual world, Jammie persistently and diligently continued to refine and improve her already considerable skills. To further refine her technique, she committed herself to diligent training sessions, working in close collaboration with her trainer to enhance her precision, increase her strength, and cultivate greater finesse in her movements. Driven by a desire for deeper connection with Comet, she pushed her artistry to new heights, aiming for technically perfect and emotionally powerful performances. With renowned dressage masters, she honed her riding, absorbing their expertise and always striving for improvement.

The relationship with Comet deepened, too. He seemed to sense the change in her, a newfound confidence and calmness that translated into a seamless partnership in the arena. Their communication was effortless, a symphony of movement, a harmonious blend of skill and instinct. He responded to her subtle cues with unwavering precision, anticipating her intentions and enhancing their performance with remarkable synchronicity. Their bond was more than a rider-horse relationship; it was a testament to their mutual respect and trust, forged in countless hours of training, shared experiences, and mutual devotion.

Her personal life also flourished. The Grand Prix victory had brought her family closer, bridging the gap that had existed before.

Once distant and reserved, her parents were now openly supportive, sharing in her joy and celebrating her achievements. They attended her competitions, offering encouragement and words of affirmation.

Her relationship with John thrived, too. He was unwavering in his support, celebrating her triumphs and grounding her amidst the whirlwind of the post-Grand Prix attention. He understood the pressure and demands and was always there, providing a steady anchor amidst the chaos.

Her friendship with Sarah remained strong, a testament to the resilience of their bond. They celebrated her victory together, sharing moments of laughter and quiet reflection. Sarah's unwavering support and understanding of Jammie's journey had been invaluable, a constant reminder that genuine connections transcend external achievements.

The Grand Prix was a pivotal turning point in Jamie's life. It wasn't simply a competition won; it was a testament to her resilience, unwavering commitment to her passion, and capacity for growth. One chapter ended, another started, bringing fresh challenges, opportunities, and a commitment to excellence. She knew the journey would continue, with its share of triumphs and setbacks. However, she felt prepared, stronger, more confident, determined.

A transformation occurred in the girl once plagued by self-doubt. The Grand Prix hadn't changed her life; it had revealed the powerful, confident, and resilient young woman she had always been, waiting to be unleashed. This triumph transcended trophies and ribbons. The future stretched before her, bright and full of promise, a testament to the unwavering spirit that had carried her through the trials and ultimately led her to success. An arduous journey yielded a rewarding destination; the future, though unclear, promises exciting discoveries. The Grand Prix was a memory, a milestone, but the journey was beginning.

Chapter 37: Relationship with Karen

The lingering tension between Jammie and Karen, a silent undercurrent throughout the Grand Prix, didn't dissipate with the last flourish of Comet's piaffe. Instead, it simmered, a low hum beneath the surface of their shared equestrian world. Once fueled by a potent cocktail of ambition and insecurity, the rivalry shifted subtly. Karen, for all her outward confidence, seemed...different. Previously bold defiance now felt brittle, near defenseless.

The beginning was subtle, marked only by a slight, almost imperceptible gesture. In the warm-up arena, someone offered a nearly hesitant nod, brief in its duration. Lost in the dazzling afterglow of her triumphant win and overwhelmed by the many post-competition interviews and celebratory functions, Jammie initially didn't perceive these slight alterations in her surroundings. However, as time went on, Karen's transformation became impossible to ignore.

One afternoon, Jammie found Karen in the tack room, meticulously cleaning her saddle, a stark contrast to her usual hurried efficiency. The air hung heavy with unspoken words, the usual competitive glare absent. Karen looked up. Her usual haughty expression softened, almost hesitant.

"Your test was... impressive," Karen finally says, her voice devoid of its usual biting sarcasm. The simple compliment hung between them, heavy and unexpected.

Jammie, surprised, managed a small smile. "Thanks. Yours was good too," she replies, surprised by the ease of the exchange. The usual sparring match of words felt absent, replaced by a strange sense of shared understanding.

Their conversations became less infrequent, less barbed. They began sharing insights about their training regimens, struggles with specific movements, and even their frustrations with their respective horses. It wasn't a sudden friendship, a more cautious thawing of the icy relationship that had defined their previous interactions. They discussed the pressures of competition, the sacrifices, and the relentless drive for perfection, revealing a shared vulnerability hidden beneath their carefully constructed public personas.

Jammie discovered a deep-seated fear of failure beneath Karen's formidable exterior, one that was mirrored in her own, albeit expressed in starkly different ways. Karen's arrogance, Jammie realized, wasn't born of genuine confidence, but a shield against her insecurities. The constant need to prove herself, to outshine everyone else, stemmed from a profound self-doubt that she fiercely guarded. Jammie saw echoes of herself in Karen, a reflection she hadn't expected.

One evening, during a quiet session in the stables, Karen confided in Jammie about the immense pressure from her family and the expectations that weighed heavily on her shoulders. Her parents, driven by ambition, pushed her relentlessly, demanding perfection, creating an environment where any mistake felt like a catastrophic failure. Jammie listened intently, recognizing the familiar ache of parental expectations, the crushing weight of living up to a family legacy.

"It's exhausting," Karen admitted, her voice barely a whisper, the carefully constructed mask finally slipping. "I want to ride because I love it, not because I have to." The raw emotion in her voice was startling, a revelation that laid bare the fragility beneath the veneer of invincibility.

This vulnerability, this honest confession, broke down the wall between them, erasing the years of rivalry and competition. Jammie empathized with Karen, understanding the immense pressure she faced and the toll it took on her spirit. Jammie realized that their competition, though intense, was ultimately a battle against their insecurities, a fight for self-worth and recognition.

In her newfound confidence and maturity, Jammie offered Karen a hand, not as a rival, but as a fellow rider who understood the struggle. They supported each other, sharing advice, celebrating each other's successes, and offering solace during setbacks.

Their conversations moved beyond mere horse talk; they shared their dreams, anxieties, and aspirations. The shared experience of intense competition, facing self-doubt, and the immense pressure of expectation forged a bond stronger than any rivalry.

This newfound camaraderie wasn't a betrayal of their competitive spirit. Despite continued rivalry and pursuit of success, their motivation shifted. It was a drive fueled not by rivalry but by mutual respect and a shared passion for their sport. They grasped competition's potential for non-destruction. Their shared journey, once defined by intense competition, was now enriched by understanding, empathy, and a shared passion for their art.

The transformation wasn't immediate; it was gradual, evolving organically through shared struggles and triumphs. It took time, patience, and a willingness to see beyond the surface. The change in Karen was remarkable. The sharp edges softened, the arrogance mellowed into a quieter self-assurance. Her bravado persisted, yet vulnerability now made her more approachable.

Their relationship, once defined by competition, became a testament to the possibility of growth, maturity, and understanding, even within the context of intense rivalry. They learned mutual appreciation, support, and genuine understanding, moving beyond outward appearances.

The shared experience of the Grand Prix, the intense pressures, and the subsequent media attention catalyzed this transformation.

The journey toward self-discovery was one they embarked upon together, and this shared path led them to a mutual respect and understanding that transcended the competitive arena. They remained rivals, of course, but the rivalry was now infused with respect, admiration, and a quiet understanding that went beyond the glitter and the glory of the Grand Prix. Their relationship had evolved beyond the competition, a testament to the power of shared experiences and a willingness to confront and overcome their internal struggles.

Their bond, forged in the crucible of intense competition, ultimately became a source of strength for both of them. They learned to appreciate the nuances of each other's riding styles, to offer constructive feedback, and to support one another's goals and aspirations. Their friendship, once unimaginable, became a valuable asset, proving that even in the most competitive environments, genuine connection and understanding can blossom.

The change in their relationship wasn't about their individual growth; it also affected their performances. Karen's riding became more fluid, more expressive, less rigid. The tension that had previously clouded her movements seemed to dissipate, replaced by a graceful ease that mirrored her newfound emotional balance.

Jammie, too, benefited from the change. The weight of her past rivalries lifted, freeing her to focus solely on her craft, allowing her to express herself with even greater artistry and precision. Their shared journey, once defined by conflict, now fuels their individual growth and artistry. Their newfound respect and camaraderie fostered an environment of mutual support, shaping their performances and solidifying their passion for the sport of dressage.

This new dynamic transformed the competitive landscape. No longer locked in a bitter rivalry, they could appreciate each other's strengths, acknowledging their achievements with genuine admiration rather than begrudging acceptance. This change didn't diminish their competitive spirit; instead, it refined it, shaping it into something more profound and meaningful. Their journey, from bitter rivals to supportive colleagues, has become an inspirational tale within their equestrian community, showcasing that growth and maturity are attainable even in the demanding landscape of professional sports.

Chapter 38: Strengthened Bonds

The Grand Prix victory felt like a lifetime ago, the whirlwind of interviews and congratulations a distant memory. Life settled back into a more familiar rhythm, the daily routine of training and schoolwork resuming its hold. But the subtle yet profound changes continued to ripple through Jammie's life. The shift in her relationship with Karen had been significant, but it was only one piece of a larger puzzle of growth and understanding.

John, ever Jammie's steadfast rock, had witnessed her transformation. He'd seen the vulnerability she'd revealed during the competition, the raw emotion that had threatened to overwhelm her. He'd also seen her newfound confidence, a quiet strength from within. Their strong relationship deepened as they shared their triumphs and struggles, with their conversations moving beyond the confines of teenage romance to encompass more profound discussions about their aspirations and fears. He understood the pressures she faced and the weight of expectations and provided a haven where she could be herself, without pretense or performance. He celebrated her victories, not as a rider, but as Jammie, her triumphs becoming shared victories within their growing connection.

One evening, after a grueling training session with Comet, Jammie found John waiting for her at the stables. He'd brought her hot chocolate, a simple gesture that spoke volumes about his understanding and care. They sat together, the scent of hay and leather filling the air, as they talked about her day. Jammie confided in him about her ongoing conversations with Karen and the surprising camaraderie they were developing. John listened patiently, offering support and insightful observations. He understood the complexities of their relationship, the way it had evolved from a bitter rivalry to a fragile yet genuine connection. He knew that Jammie's growth extended beyond her achievements in the arena; it was a holistic transformation encompassing all aspects of her life.

Their conversations often extended beyond dressage. They talked about their dreams for the future, their hopes, and their ambitions. John's unwavering support gave Jammie the courage to explore her passions beyond the confines of the equestrian world. He encouraged her artistic pursuits, her love of writing, and her quiet moments of reflection. Their bond became a source of strength, a refuge from the pressures of competition and the expectations that weighed heavily upon her. His presence constantly reminded her that success meant more than ribbons and trophies; it meant personal growth, self-discovery, and strong human connection.

Beyond John, Jammie's friendships also deepened. Her relationship with Chloe, her longtime friend and fellow equestrian, thrived amidst the shared experience of navigating the complexities of adolescence and the challenges of competitive riding. They celebrated each other's triumphs and offered support during setbacks, their bond strengthened by their shared passion and mutual understanding. Chloe, unlike some of their classmates who found the equestrian world intimidating, understood Jammie's dedication and passion. She didn't judge her for the pressures or sacrifices she faced.

Their discussions included more than just horses. Their conversation covered boys, school, dreams, and the future. They marked birthdays, exchanged secrets, and provided unwavering support when times were hard. They offered Jammie sanctuary from cutthroat competition and a space for unburdened self-expression. Jammie found the genuine, rivalry-free connection invaluable; it was a stabilizing influence in her life, a welcome change from the competitive, stable environment.

Jammie's friendship with Liam, another rider in their stable, provided a different perspective. Jammie found comfort and direction in Liam's calm demeanor and encouraging words as he navigated the emotional challenges of competition and personal growth. The pressure he felt wasn't from family or coaches, but from his own self-imposed expectations. In her circle of friends, he offered a different dynamic, a contrast to the intensely competitive friendships. He offered a place for reflection and development that went beyond typical horse discussions.

Initially intimidated by Jammie's success, the girls in their class approached her with questions and genuine interest. Discovering Jammie's softer side fostered a deeper friendship, replacing initial admiration. They realized she wasn't some unattainable star; she was a normal girl with incredible passion and talent. They shared laughter, secrets, and hopes for the future; their conversations enriched Jammie's life, providing a much-needed escape from the pressure of the equestrian world.

The newfound confidence and maturity that had blossomed from her journey extended beyond her relationship with Karen and her romantic life. It pervaded all aspects of her life. She navigated the complexities of school and friendships with a renewed sense of purpose and self-awareness. Her art flourished, reflecting her newfound emotional depth and self-acceptance. Her writing became more expressive, her words flowing freely, reflecting the inner strength she had discovered.

The strengthened bonds within her life weren't merely collateral benefits of her success in the competition. They were integral to her growth, providing the support, understanding, and encouragement she needed to navigate the challenges and triumphs of her equestrian journey. They served as a reminder that success wasn't a solitary pursuit, but a journey shared with those who believed in her, loved her, and supported her unconditionally.

The support from her friends, the unwavering love from John, and the surprising camaraderie with Karen created a safety net, allowing Jammie to push her boundaries, to take risks, and to embrace vulnerability. This web of supportive relationships, both within and outside the equestrian world, didn't enhance her life; it allowed her to thrive, flourish, and truly embrace the power of genuine human connection. It transformed her, not as a rider, but as a person, allowing her to approach the future with a confidence that stemmed from a deep sense of self and strong, meaningful relationships. The bonds she forged, both old and new, became the foundation upon which she built her future, proving that the most powerful victories are often the ones celebrated beyond the boundaries of the competition arena. The journey, far from being over, had only begun, a journey she was prepared to face, empowered by the unwavering support of those who mattered most.

Chapter 39: Future Aspirations

The quiet confidence that had settled over Jammie wasn't merely a post-Grand Prix glow; it was a fundamental shift, a deep-seated change that permeated every aspect of her life. The victory hadn't been about winning a ribbon; it had been a victory over her self-doubt, a testament to her resilience. And with this newfound self-assurance came a clarity of purpose, a vision for her future that extended far beyond the confines of the dressage arena.

Initially, her future seemed inextricably linked to horses. The thought of life without Comet, her magnificent Andalusian stallion, was almost unimaginable. He was more than a horse; he was a partner, a confidante, a mirror reflecting her growth and evolution. The idea of competing at the highest level, perhaps even representing her country one day, flickered in her mind, a tantalizing possibility fueled by her recent success. She envisioned herself at the Olympic Games, the crowd's roar, the competition's intensity, the sheer exhilaration of performing at the pinnacle of her sport.

But she aspired to more than just the competitive world. The Grand Prix victory had given her a platform and voice, and she was exploring how to use that influence. She had always loved writing, finding solace and expression in the written word. The pressure of the competition had inspired her to keep a detailed journal, in which she documented her thoughts, fears, and triumphs. Raw and honest, these entries became the foundation for a larger project—a memoir about her journey as a dressage rider. It wasn't a chronicle of wins and losses but a story of self-discovery, overcoming adversity, and finding strength in vulnerability. She envisioned this memoir reaching other young equestrians, offering them solace, inspiration, and perhaps even the courage to pursue their dreams with unwavering determination.

Her artistic talents, previously relegated to the sidelines, blossomed under the nurturing light of her newfound confidence. She incorporated her experiences into her artwork, transforming her emotions and the breathtaking beauty of the equestrian world into striking visual representations. The vibrant colors of the stables, the fluid elegance of Comet's movement, the tension and excitement of the competition—all found their way onto her canvases. She experimented with different mediums, exploring oils, watercolors, and charcoal, each offering a unique perspective and emotional resonance. She dreamed of one day having her art exhibition, showcasing her work to a broader audience and expressing her unique vision of the world through the lens of her passion for horses.

Beyond her creative pursuits, Jammie also considered the possibility of coaching. Sharing her expertise and experience with other riders was something she always enjoyed. Recognizing the opportunity to mentor younger riders, she aimed to guide them through competitive dressage, sharing her hard-earned wisdom. She imparted technical skills and the importance of mental strength, persistence, and self-assurance. In her vision, she played a key role in developing future riders, instilling the passion and commitment she embodied.

Jammie didn't focus solely on her ambitions. She also recognized the importance of supporting the equestrian community. She witnessed firsthand the stable owners, trainers, and volunteers. By improving others' lives, she hoped to give back to her community. Helping underprivileged children ride, volunteering at local stables, or starting a foundation for young equestrians lacking resources were all options she considered. Her wish to help others showed her humility and thankfulness, proving that she knew her success wasn't only because of her.

John's relationship with her also fueled her ambitions. By consistently backing her ambitions, he inspired her to reach for the stars, driving her to pursue her dreams passionately and relentlessly. Recognizing the significance of her personal life and creative outlets, he understood her need for a balanced lifestyle. He was a perpetual wellspring of inspiration, always motivating her to challenge herself and find potential outside her comfort zone in competition. Discussions went beyond immediate plans; they explored their intertwined yet independent futures and long-term goals

Their shared dreams extended beyond the immediate future. They envisioned a future where they could live near the stables, creating a home that would serve as a haven for both of them and a space to welcome their friends and family. They discussed building a life around their shared passion, supporting each other's goals while ensuring a firm foundation for their life together. This shared vision provided Jammie with a solid anchor, security, and a sense of belonging. It reminded her she wasn't alone in her journey, that someone loved her unconditionally, celebrated her victories, and comforted her in her setbacks.

Even her complex relationship with Karen had undergone a surprising transformation. Their newfound respect showed genuine appreciation for each other's abilities. Jammie saw Karen's ambition and drive as a reflection of her unwavering dedication. Karen recognized Jammie's skill and the quiet strength that had enabled her to overcome her self-doubt. Their shared experience in the competitive world forged a bond based on mutual understanding and respect, a foundation for future collaboration.

They discussed potential coaching opportunities, sharing their expertise to help inexperienced riders and nurture the next generation of talented equestrians. Their paths might diverge in some areas, yet their shared passion for dressage and mutual respect created a platform for potential collaboration.

Jammie realized that the future wasn't a single, predetermined path, but a vast landscape of opportunities, waiting to be explored. Her ambitions were diverse, her goals multifaceted, each reflecting a different facet of her personality and passion for horses. The Grand Prix victory had been a significant milestone, but it was merely a stepping stone on a much larger and more enriching journey.

She was excited about the possibilities ahead, confident in her abilities, and empowered by the support of her friends, family, and her beloved Comet. The future wasn't a destination; it was an adventure, a journey filled with challenges and triumphs, a tapestry woven with her dreams, her passions, and the unwavering love and support of those around her. The journey had only begun, and Jammie was ready to embrace every exhilarating moment.

Chapter 40: Continued Growth

Jammie and Comet cantered across the sprawling fields surrounding the stables. The crisp fall air nipped at her cheeks. The Grand Prix victory felt like a distant dream, yet its impact resonated in every stride. Comet took in her heart's newfound lightness. The change wasn't about ribbons and accolades; it was a fundamental shift in her self-perception, a blossoming confidence that permeated every aspect of her life. She no longer saw limitations; she saw possibilities.

Her memoir project progressed steadily. The initial journal entries, raw and emotional outpourings during the stressful period leading up to the competition, evolved into a structured narrative. With meticulous care, she shaped each sentence, interweaving her experiences, vivid descriptions of horses and competitions, and the complex emotions that motivated her. She was adamant about not recounting her journey.

She pictured her book, offering comfort and guidance to inexperienced riders, navigating insecurities and dreams, on bookstore shelves. The dedication she poured into this project went beyond mere writing; it was self-expression, a therapeutic process that solidified her growth and understanding. She meticulously researched publishing options and even outlined a potential marketing strategy, eager to share her story with the world.

Her artistic pursuits flourished alongside her writing. The vibrant colors of her paintings reflected the kaleidoscope of emotions she had experienced. One canvas depicted the tense anticipation before a Grand Prix performance, with the horses' breath misting in the cold air and the riders' faces reflecting a mixture of nervousness and determination. Another showcased Comet's raw power and elegance in full flight, his coat gleaming under the sunlight, his movements a symphony of grace and strength. Drawing inspiration from both the elegance of the equestrian world and the beauty of the landscapes surrounding her cherished stables, she enthusiastically experimented with a diverse range of artistic styles. In her artwork, she skillfully blended abstract elements, transforming the elusive and intangible emotions experienced during her personal journey into a vivid and vibrant tapestry of visual representations.

Through the innovative use of mixed media, specifically incorporating collage elements into her paintings, she crafted complex and layered works of art that powerfully mirrored the multifaceted nature of her personal and artistic development. The thought of exhibiting her work, of sharing her artistic vision with the world, filled her with exhilaration and a renewed sense of purpose. She began researching galleries and art fairs, investigating the possibility of hosting her exhibition — a dream that seemed audacious yet within her grasp.

Coaching provided Jammie with an additional platform to share her passion and knowledge. At the local riding school, she started by patiently guiding younger riders through the basics of dressage in her volunteer role. Surprisingly, she discovered a natural talent for teaching, connecting with students and inspiring them to achieve great things. She adapted her approach to each rider's individual needs and challenges. She highlighted the importance of technical riding skills, self-belief, resilience, and.

As a mentor, not an instructor, she saw her role as nurturing their passion for the sport and guiding them through competitive riding complexities. The joy she derived from teaching was immense, a testament to her transformation from an insecure teenager to a confident and capable young woman. The experience deepened her understanding of the sport, challenging her to articulate her knowledge and refine her technique.

Her commitment to giving back to the equestrian community grew organically. At local horse shows, she volunteered, assisting with various tasks, from preparing the arena to managing the awards ceremony. Driven by her newfound influence, she advocated for animal welfare and supported inexperienced riders from disadvantaged backgrounds. She began planning a fundraising event to raise money for a local charity that provided riding lessons to children with disabilities. She expected difficulty, yet her resolve stemmed from affecting lives.

Giving back encompassed far more than charitable contributions; it was a demonstration of deep-seated values and a commitment to positive change.

Her journey of service provided a new perspective, reinforcing her core values and the significance of humility and gratitude.

Jammie's relationship with John thrived amidst her busy schedule.

He was her unwavering support system, celebrating her triumphs and providing comfort during her moments of doubt. They spent hours discussing her ambitions, planning her next steps, and dreaming about their shared future. Helped her balance her various pursuits, ensuring that she didn't overextend herself and that she prioritized her well-being. Recognizing her profound dedication to both writing and art, he fully grasped her requirement for creative expression. Their relationship was strictly platonic; he was not her boyfriend. With every passing day, their relationship flourished, nurtured by the common dreams they held dear and the unwavering respect they showed each other.

They started planning a small celebration, not to mark the Grand Prix victory, but to celebrate the broader scope of Jammie's growth and evolution. This journey transformed her into the confident, passionate young woman she had become.

Even her relationship with Karen had changed. Their shared passion for dressage and the mutual respect forged after the Grand Prix had grown into a genuine friendship. They exchanged ideas, offered each other encouragement, and even explored collaborating on future projects, from co-coaching novice riders to organizing small equestrian events. This new dynamic broadened Jammie's perspective and deepened her appreciation for the diversity of talent and experience within the equestrian community. They recognized that success in dressage wasn't about individual achievement, but also collaboration and mutual support. This unexpected friendship enriched Jammie's life, demonstrating that even the strongest rivalries could pave the way for meaningful connections and shared growth.

Jammie reflected on her incredible journey as the year drew to a close. The Grand Prix victory was pivotal, but it also served as a stepping stone on a path filled with endless possibilities. She was no longer defined by her self-doubt or the pressure to live up to her family's legacy. She forged her identity, a unique blend of talent, resilience, and unwavering determination. Her future stretched before her, a vast and exciting landscape of opportunities, waiting to be explored. She embraced this future with open arms, confident in her abilities and grateful for the love and support of those around her. The journey had only begun, and Jammie was ready to ride towards the horizon, her heart full of hope and her spirit soaring.

The quiet confidence that had blossomed within her wasn't merely a fleeting emotion; it was a deep-seated strength that would guide her through all the challenges and triumphs ahead. The future was a thrilling adventure, a testament to her perseverance and a reflection of her unwavering passion for the equestrian world. She prepared, not for another contest, but for a life rich with meaning.

Chapter 41: Overcoming Self-Doubt

The lingering scent of sawdust and leather still clung to her clothes, a faint reminder of the countless hours she had spent in the stables, honing her skills and battling her inner demons. The Grand Prix victory hadn't magically erased her self-doubt; it had merely chipped away at its formidable walls, revealing the strength she hadn't known she possessed. The journey wasn't about achieving a flawless performance; it was about the relentless pursuit of improvement, the constant struggle against self-doubt and self-criticism, and the unwavering commitment to her passion.

One particularly blustery afternoon, while working with a young, hesitant rider at the local stables, a familiar wave of self-doubt washed over Jammie. The girl, barely ten years old, struggled to maintain her balance on the pony, her eyes wide with apprehension. A sudden memory flashed—herself at that age, gripped by the same anxieties and fear of failure. She remembered the crushing weight of expectations, the constant comparisons to her older siblings, and the relentless pressure to uphold the family legacy. The old insecurities threatened to resurface momentarily, undermining her hard-won confidence.

But this time, something was different. Instead of retreating into herself, Jammie drew upon her experiences. Her voice, soft yet firm, was a calming influence as she calmly approached the inexperienced rider, reassuring them with her steady presence. Rather than offering empty reassurances, she remained silent, recognizing the ineffectiveness of hollow promises.

The transformation was gradual, subtle, but undeniable. It wasn't a sudden, dramatic shift, but a slow, steady evolution. The self-doubt didn't vanish overnight; it lingered, a persistent whisper in the background, but its power had diminished. She learned to acknowledge its presence without letting it dictate her actions. She embraced the imperfection, admitting that her journey wouldn't always be smooth, and that setbacks were inevitable.

Her writing became a crucial tool in this process of self-discovery. Her memoir wasn't a recounting of her triumphs, but a raw and honest exploration of her vulnerabilities, fears, and struggles. She delved into the depths of her self-doubt, dissecting its origins, understanding its mechanics, and gradually stripping it of its power. Each word she wrote was a step towards reclaiming her narrative, and silencing the voices of self-criticism.

The act of writing forced her to confront her insecurities head-on. It wasn't easy; there were moments of doubt, moments where she wanted to abandon the project, to bury her vulnerabilities under layers of carefully constructed prose. But she persevered, driven by the need to share her story, to offer hope and inspiration to others who had walked a similar path. The process was cathartic, therapeutic, a way of exorcising her demons and emerging stronger, more resilient, and more self-aware.

Her artistic pursuits mirrored this journey. Her paintings, once dominated by muted tones and somber landscapes, now burst with vibrant colors, reflecting the transformation within her. She experimented with bold strokes, capturing the raw emotion of her struggles, the exhilarating highs of her victories, and the quiet moments of self-reflection. Her art was an extension of her self-healing, a visual testament to her growth and resilience.

Even her coaching style reflected her evolved perspective. She had ceased her instruction in the technical elements of dressage, focusing her energies elsewhere. Highlighting self-compassion, she underscored the value of minor victories and reframing setbacks as learning experiences. Her classroom became a haven where students felt safe to be vulnerable, supported by mutual respect and encouragement. Her approach became less about achieving perfection and more about fostering a love for the sport, building confidence, and nurturing a deep connection between rider and horse.

While working late on her memoir one evening, Jammie paused, gazing at the moonlit stables. The place's familiar calm brought unprecedented peace. She had reached a point where she could acknowledge her self-doubt without being overwhelmed. It was a part of her, but it no longer defined her. She was a work in progress, constantly evolving, learning, and continually pushing herself beyond her perceived limitations.

Her relationship with John also deepened, their bond strengthened by her newfound self-assurance. He didn't dismiss her doubts; instead, he listened patiently, offering unwavering support and encouragement. He celebrated her victories as accomplishments in the equestrian world and triumphs over her internal battles. He understood the depths of her emotional journey and validated her feelings, providing a solid foundation for her growth.

Her interactions with Karen, her former rival, also transformed. Their shared passion for dressage and mutual respect forged a genuine friendship. They collaborated on workshops for inexperienced riders, combining their expertise and providing a unique blend of instruction and emotional support. This collaboration cemented Jammie's growth and her acceptance of her strengths and weaknesses. She learned that competition didn't have to be a zero-sum game; it could be a catalyst for mutual growth, collaboration, and shared learning. It fostered community and solidarity.

The winter brought with it the quiet satisfaction of a job well done. Her memoir was finally complete, a testament to her resilience, a beacon of hope for aspiring riders everywhere. She scheduled her paintings for a local exhibition, bravely stepping into the world of public art. The response exceeded her wildest expectations; her art resonated with viewers, reminding them of their struggles and triumphs. The positive feedback validated her journey and solidified her self-belief.

As springtime sprung forth, it carried with it a revitalizing feeling of renewed purpose, a breath of fresh air for all. With a passion for dressage and a desire to empower the next generation, she began mentoring a group of aspiring young riders, sharing her extensive experience, encouraging them to embrace their individuality and overcome any fears they might have while riding. Jammie discovered a profound and lasting sense of purpose and satisfaction through her dedication to mentoring and teaching others. They eliminated her from the competition.

The warmth of a successful summer enveloped everything. The critical response to her recently published book was incredibly positive, and, adding to her success, her paintings sold out at an impressive rate, exceeding all expectations. This wasn't about others' approval, but her own sense of fulfillment—knowing her journey mattered, her story connected, and she'd had an impact. The culmination of years of hard work, dedication, and self-discovery was this.

Looking back, Jammie realized that overcoming self-doubt wasn't a single event, but a continuous process, a lifelong journey of self-discovery and growth. The Grand Prix victory was pivotal, but it was merely one step on a much larger journey. She learned that self-doubt was not the enemy, but a challenge to be acknowledged, understood, and ultimately transcended. It was in facing her insecurities and embracing her vulnerabilities that she truly found her strength, resilience, and purpose. The journey had shaped her, molded her, and strengthened her and was wiser than she had ever imagined. The girl who once trembled under the pressure of competition had become a confident and compassionate leader, inspiring others to pursue their dreams with courage and determination. And that, she realized, was her most significant victory.

Chapter 42: The Importance of Support

The quiet hum of the refrigerator was the only sound in the kitchen as Jammie stirred her chamomile tea, the steam momentarily obscuring her face. The memory of Karen's warm smile, shared during their recent collaborative workshop for inexperienced riders, still brought a smile to her lips. It had been an unexpected but profoundly positive experience, starkly contrasting with their earlier rivalry. Unexpected sources, initially perceived as obstacles, revealed the true power of support, eclipsing that of romantic partners and family.

With her unwavering self-confidence and sharp wit, Karen initially seemed the antithesis of Jammie's self-doubt. Yet, their shared passion for dressage, stripped bare of the competitive pressure, created a foundation for mutual respect and genuine connection. Working together, they found common ground, not in the technical aspects of the sport but in the shared challenges of overcoming personal insecurities and the pressures of pursuing excellence. Jammie realized that actual competition wasn't about tearing others down; it was about striving for personal best, pushing boundaries, and celebrating the achievements of others. Karen's unwavering support and belief in Jammie's abilities had been instrumental in her self-acceptance.

John provided constant, unwavering support to her throughout her journey. Instead of offering empty platitudes or dismissing her fears, he showed genuine understanding and concern. His celebrations of her dressage wins weren't just about the sport; they were about her overcoming personal struggles. He knew how emotionally taxing the pursuit of perfection could be. Her self-criticism eroded her self-confidence, but his steadfast support guided her through difficult times. Amid life's storms, he was her unwavering source of strength and calm.

Romantic love and newfound friendships did not solely compose the support system that profoundly shaped Jammie's journey.

Her family had initially been a source of immense pressure, but they had inadvertently taught her the importance of resilience and hard work. While their expectations had been demanding, they had also instilled in her a deep-seated love for dressage and an unwavering dedication to her craft. Their legacy, which burdened her with self-doubt, ultimately fueled her passion and drove her to achieve her goals.

The acceptance of her parents' support, though initially fraught with tension and resentment, became a cornerstone of her personal growth. She understood their actions, not as personal attacks, but as manifestations of their anxieties and desires for her success. This realization enabled Jammie to cultivate a more balanced perspective on their relationship, alleviating the burden of their expectations and transforming their dynamic into one of mutual understanding and support. This shift allowed her to receive their support without feeling suffocated by it.

Her younger siblings, initially viewed as a source of comparison and competition, had become allies on her journey. They understood her struggles, her triumphs, and her vulnerabilities. They offered a unique perspective, free of the expectations and pressures faced by her parents. Their shared experience of family life, with its unique challenges, forged a bond of understanding that strengthened her sense of belonging and self-worth.

Beyond her immediate circle, Jammie found support in unexpected places. The inexperienced riders she coached at the local stables, each facing their challenges and insecurities, reminded her of her journey, reinforcing her belief in the power of self-compassion and the importance of celebrating minor victories. Their vulnerability mirrored her past, creating a connection and mutual understanding that enriched her teaching and coaching style. Their growth became her own, a continuous source of inspiration and reassurance.

Her writing itself became a powerful source of support. Transforming her experiences into words, weaving her vulnerability into a narrative, was a cathartic experience. It wasn't an act of self-expression; it was a process of self-discovery, a journey of healing and reconciliation. Writing her memoir wasn't simply about documenting her life; it was about making sense of her experiences, transforming her pain into understanding, and ultimately, empowerment.

The feedback she received in her memoir, both from friends and strangers, reinforced the importance of her journey. The readers who connected with her experiences and found comfort and hope in her story provided an unexpected layer of support. Their gratitude and encouragement were a powerful testament to the value of sharing one's vulnerability, strengthening her resolve to continue sharing her experiences. The exhibition of her paintings provided a comparable feeling of approval and confirmation of her artistic merit.

Seeing the positive public response to her artwork, she felt a strong connection between her creative work and the viewers, which reaffirmed her self-belief and strengthened her conviction in art's power as a means of self-expression and healing. The considerable positive feedback significantly altered her artistic journey, powerfully affecting her confidence and artistic expression. Uncertainty and self-doubt did little to deter her; instead, the experience solidified her conviction and determination to pursue her passions relentlessly.

Even the horses themselves played a role in Jammie's support system. During moments of self-doubt, the unwavering trust, quiet companionship, and unspoken connection between rider and horse offered comfort and strength. The feeling of being understood and accepted by a creature so different yet deeply connected, even in silence, gave Jammie a sense of peace. The relationship with each horse mirrored her journey of self-discovery, growth, trust, and mutual respect.

Jammie's journey wasn't about overcoming her self-doubt; it was about recognizing the importance of a strong support network, about understanding that strength isn't just about individual resilience, but also about the power of connection and shared experience. My journey involved realizing that vulnerability isn't weakness. In these connections and supportive relationships, Jammie truly found the strength to face her fears, embrace her vulnerabilities, and ultimately, achieve her dreams. The power of support wasn't about receiving help; it was about actively building and nurturing relationships, fostering a sense of belonging, and creating a community of shared experiences and mutual growth. Human connection, not riding, was the lesson learned.

Chapter 43: Embracing Challenges

The Grand Prix loomed, a behemoth of expectation and pressure. Despite the newfound confidence gleaned from her burgeoning friendships and John's unwavering support, Jammie still felt the tremor of fear deep in her gut. It wasn't a fear of failure, exactly, not anymore. A deeper, more instinctive dread fueled her; she feared failure, unable to uphold her family's legacy. This fear wasn't rational; it was a ghost from her past, a phantom limb of self-doubt that refused to be silenced.

The morning of the competition dawned crisp and clear, the air vibrating with a nervous energy that mirrored her own. The stables were abuzz with activity—the rhythmic clip-clop of horses' hooves, the hushed conversations of riders and grooms, the occasional sharp cry of instruction. Jammie found herself strangely calm amidst the chaos. The years of rigorous training and the countless hours spent honing her skills had prepared her not only for the physical demands of the competition, but also for the emotional turmoil that accompanied it. She had learned to channel her nerves, to transform anxiety into focused energy.

Her first ride was a blur of controlled movements, precise transitions, and the unwavering connection with her horse, Apollo. Apollo, a magnificent Friesian stallion, responded to her commands with effortless grace, his powerful strides echoing her determination. The judges awarded decent, though unimpressive, scores. Jammie knew she could have done better; a momentary lapse in concentration during the extended trot had cost her precious points. Instead of succumbing to disappointment, she focused on what she had learned. This mistake, far from shameful, proved instructive; it showed that top riders are fallible. It was how they responded to those mistakes that truly defined them.

The second round presented a unique set of challenges. The arena was larger, the atmosphere more intense, the pressure palpable.

Her erstwhile rival, Karen, was performing flawlessly, her confidence radiating through the arena like a beacon. Jammie, instead of feeling intimidated, found herself inspired. Karen's performance served as a reminder of her capabilities, a testament to the power of dedication and hard work. She channeled Karen's strength, not as a competitive force, but as a source of motivation.

This time, Jammie was flawless. She and Apollo moved as one, a seamless blend of power and grace, their performance a testament to their unwavering bond and Jammie's mastery of the sport. The crowd erupted in applause. A wave of sound washed over her, momentarily silencing the inner critic that had plagued her for so long. The judges' scores were extraordinary, exceeding even her expectations. It wasn't about the technical aspects of her ride, but about the emotional maturity she had displayed, the resilience she had showed in the face of adversity.

The subsequent days were a whirlwind of competition, camaraderie, and self-reflection. Jammie engaged in thoughtful conversations with other riders, sharing experiences, offering support, and receiving it in return. The competition wasn't about individual achievement but about the shared journey, the collective striving for excellence, and the mutual respect among competitors. The challenges they faced were not unique to her; they were universal experiences, shared by all who dared to pursue their passions with unwavering dedication.

She reflected on the journey, not just the Grand Prix competition, but her entire life. The initial pressure from her family, the intense rivalry with Karen, the self-doubt that had threatened to derail her dreams—these experiences had shaped her, molded her, and strengthened her. She had learned to embrace challenges, not as insurmountable obstacles, but as opportunities for growth. She understood self-compassion's importance, plus forgiveness's power—for herself and others.

The Grand Prix served not as a mere competition, but as a crucible, forging her character, refining her skills, and illuminating her future path, revealing her true potential. In confronting her challenges, she unexpectedly uncovered a previously unknown strength: a remarkable resilience coupled with a steadfast determination she never realized she possessed. Over time, she developed a strong reliance on her intuition and instincts, understanding that embracing her vulnerabilities was a key component to her personal growth. She discovered that genuine success wasn't about achieving flawless perfection, but about embracing a journey of consistent self-improvement, ongoing personal growth, and the acceptance of oneself, flaws and all.

The aftermath of the competition was a mix of relief and exhilaration. The pressure had lifted, but the memories and lessons learned would remain etched in her mind forever. She had achieved success, not in the arena, but in her personal growth. She had overcome her self-doubt, embraced her vulnerabilities, and discovered a strength she never knew she possessed.

The journey, however, didn't end with the Grand Prix. It was an ongoing process, a continuous cycle of growth, challenges, and self-discovery. Each competition, lesson, and setback would be a stepping stone on her journey toward her goals. The experience reinforced the importance of embracing challenges rather than shying away from them. In confronting these difficulties head-on, she discovered her true capabilities, resilience, and capacity for growth.

The support system she'd cultivated—John, Karen, her family, her friends, even her horses—remained crucial. They weren't merely a crutch, but integral parts of her journey, each contributing to her growth in unique and invaluable ways. Her lessons extended far beyond the equestrian world; they were lessons in life: perseverance, resilience, the importance of embracing vulnerability, and the power of human connection.

She realized that winning or achieving a certain skill level didn't solely define success; The competition had highlighted the importance of celebrating her achievements and those of others. It had taught her the value of collaboration, mutual support, and the power of shared experience. Large and small victories weren't about her accomplishments, but about the collective spirit, mutual support, and collaborative journey.

The lessons extended beyond the competition itself; they penetrated her daily life. She applied the same principles of resilience, determination, and self-compassion to other areas of her life, including her academic pursuits, relationships, and personal development. The ability to embrace challenges, learn from setbacks, and adapt to changing circumstances became a cornerstone of her character. It was a testament to her ability to transform adversity into opportunities for personal growth and use challenges as stepping stones toward achieving her goals.

Her journey wasn't a linear progression toward success but a complex tapestry woven with threads of triumph and failure, joy and sorrow, self-doubt, and unwavering self-belief. The story was not merely about achieving excellence in dressage; it was a narrative of self-discovery, a testament to the power of resilience, support, and the transformative nature of embracing challenges. It resonated deeply with others, inspiring them to embrace their vulnerabilities and pursue their dreams with courage and unwavering determination.

And that, Jammie realized, was a victory far greater than any trophy or medal. The valid reward lay not in the accolades, but in personal growth, self-discovery, and a profound understanding of herself and her capacity for strength. The journey had transformed her from a talented but insecure, inexperienced rider into a confident, resilient, and compassionate individual, ready to face whatever challenges life throws her way.

Chapter 44: Defining Success

I felt the ribbon-Dressage ceremony was strangely anticlimactic. The champagne tasted flat; the congratulations echoing hollowly in the celebratory buzz. Standing beside Apollo, who was calmly munching on a carrot, Jammie felt a sense of disconnection. The Grand Prix had ended; she had performed exceptionally, exceeding her expectations. She had earned accolades, praise, even envy. Yet, the overwhelming feeling wasn't triumph; it was a quiet introspection, ...something missing.

It wasn't the lack of external validation. The judges' scores, the admiring glances, and the celebratory texts from John and her friends were tangible markers of success. But they didn't fill the void. She realized then, amidst the confetti and the clinking glasses, that her definition of success had been flawed.

For years, success had been synonymous with winning, achieving the highest scores, and outshining her rivals, particularly Karen. It was about living up to the expectations laid upon her by her family's legacy, a legacy that had weighed heavily on her young shoulders. She had chased the phantom of perfection, driven by external pressures rather than internal motivation. The Grand Prix victory, while significant, felt hollow because it hadn't stemmed from a genuine, self-driven pursuit of excellence. It confirmed external, not internal, aspects.

This realization was a turning point. The journey to the Grand Prix had been a crucible, refining her equestrian skills and understanding of herself. She dissected her feelings and unravel the complexities of her ambitions. The external pressure from her family, initially a source of anxiety, had inadvertently shaped her tenacity and discipline. While initially fueled by competition, her rivalry with Karen had evolved into grudging respect and a shared understanding of the dedication required to excel in the demanding world of dressage. Self-doubt, a persistent inner critic, unexpectedly spurred introspection and growth.

Upon reflection, she understood that while the Grand Prix win was a significant achievement, her personal transformation represented an even more profound and meaningful victory. No longer consumed by fear and self-doubt, she transformed from an inexperienced rider to one who embraced challenges, self-compassion, and continuous growth. She'd mastered listening to her gut, trusting her instincts, and celebrating her wins and those of her riding companions. She realized competition was less about winning and more about personal best and the collective journey.

The lessons extended beyond the arena. She recognized the parallel between the rigorous training and discipline of dressage and the dedication required in her academic life. The same focus, perseverance, and self-belief that had propelled her success in equestrian sports now served as a foundation for her educational pursuits. Her relationships, too, benefited from her newfound self-awareness. She communicated more openly, expressed her feelings more honestly, and offered unwavering support to her friends and family. Her resilience to the horse became her strength in navigating personal challenges. She learned to forgive herself for past mistakes, embracing her vulnerabilities as strengths rather than weaknesses.

The post-Grand Prix period was not a rest period, but a consolidation and expansion period. She continued her training, pushing herself to refine her skills, but with a renewed sense of purpose. The focus shifted from external validation to internal fulfillment. Each practice session focused on improving her technique and deepening her connection with Apollo, forging a stronger bond of understanding and trust.

Her relationship with Karen also evolved. The fierce rivalry softened, giving way to a mutual respect for their shared passion. They exchanged advice, share training techniques, and support each other's progress. They realized their shared pursuit of excellence had created a stronger bond than any competitive spirit. The journey to the Grand Prix had not only tested their skills but had also revealed the profound power of human connection.

Jammie started coaching younger riders, finding fulfillment in nurturing the next generation of equestrians. She shared her experiences, offering guidance and encouragement, drawing

parallels between the challenges faced in the arena and the
Struggles faced in life. Success, she stressed, was a journey, not a destination, requiring self-belief, resilience, and perseverance. She stressed the importance of self-compassion and forgiveness, enabling them to navigate inevitable setbacks with grace and maturity.

She recognized that genuine success was not about achieving perfection, but about striving for continuous self-improvement. It was about embracing challenges as opportunities for growth, learning from mistakes, and celebrating every step of the journey. She found joy in connecting with her horse and feeling harmony and trust between them. The Grand Prix victory had been a milestone, a marker of achievement, but it was one moment in a lifelong journey of learning, growth, and self-discovery.

This new perspective resonated deeply with her. Winning wasn't the point; It was about her impact on others, the connections she forged, the lessons she learned, and the inner strength she cultivated. She realized that the accurate measure of her success lay not in trophies or accolades but in the richness of her experiences, the depth of her relationships, and the unwavering pursuit of her passion. And as she looked out at the sunset, Apollo gently nuzzling her hand. She knew that her journey, her definition of success, had only begun. It was a journey of continuous growth, embracing challenges, and celebrating not just achievements, but the constant process of striving towards her full potential. This potential extended far beyond the confines of the dressage arena. The Grand Prix wasn't the end; it was a beginning, a new chapter in the ongoing story of her life, a story she was now writing with a newfound confidence, clarity, and a profound understanding of what genuine success truly meant. The accolades were a testament to her hard work and dedication. Still, the real victory lived within her, in the resilience, compassion, and unwavering spirit she had discovered along the way. This inner victory, this profound sense of self-discovery and personal growth, was a far greater reward than any external validation could ever provide. She carried a victory within her, a source of strength and inspiration, a guiding light that illuminated her path forward. She continued to tread with courage, grace, and a renewed understanding of what it meant to succeed.

Chapter 45: Finding Balance

Walking Apollo along familiar trails bordering the stables, the crisp fall air nipped at Jammie's cheeks. The Grand Prix victory felt like a distant dream, a vivid memory fading into the tapestry of her life. The initial euphoria had subsided, replaced by quiet contentment — a settled peace she hadn't known before. She had achieved something remarkable, exceeding her expectations. Yet, the victory felt less like a triumphant peak and more like a stepping stone, a solid foundation to build her future.

This newfound equilibrium wasn't about abandoning her passion for dressage; instead, it was about integrating it seamlessly into the broader context of her life. For so long, she had allowed her riding to define her, to consume her thoughts and emotions. Fueled by external pressure and internal insecurities, the relentless pursuit of perfection had created an imbalance — a lopsided existence where everything else paled compared to her equestrian ambitions. Now, her life's richness surpassed arena limitations.

Her academic life, which had once been a secondary concern, flourished. The discipline and focus she had cultivated through years of rigorous training translated directly into her studies. She approached her assignments with the same unwavering determination she applied to her dressage routines, finding a satisfying collaboration between her intellectual pursuits and her passion for horses. She discovered a profound sense of accomplishment not only in winning ribbons but also in mastering complex equations, delving into the depths of literature, and understanding the intricacies of history.

Her relationships deepened, too. John, her boyfriend, had been a constant source of support, offering unwavering encouragement even when her self-doubt threatened to consume her. He understood her passion, her dedication, and the sacrifices she made to pursue her dreams. Once strained by the demands of her training, their relationship became a source of strength and stability. He celebrated her victories as equestrian achievements and a testament to her resilience, perseverance, and unwavering spirit. Their conversations extended beyond the triumphs and tribulations of the dressage world, encompassing shared interests, common goals, and an unspoken understanding that strengthened their bond.

Her friendships also blossomed. Once viewed through the lens of competition, the girls from the stable became loyal friends. They shared their experiences, fears, and aspirations, creating a supportive network that transcended the rivalries of the arena. They celebrated each other's successes, offering comfort during times of struggle, and fostering a camaraderie that extended beyond their shared equestrian passion. The intense focus on winning had previously blinded her to the value of genuine connection, but now, she relished these friendships, recognizing their importance in her overall well-being.

Even her relationship with Karen had undergone a transformation. The animosity, born of intense competition, had mellowed into a grudging respect, acknowledging their shared dedication and passion. They shared tips and techniques, offering one another support and encouragement. The shared experience of striving for excellence created a stronger bond than their initial rivalry. Once a battleground, the arena became a shared space where they celebrated each other's accomplishments and offered solace during setbacks. They understood each other's sacrifices, dedication, and relentless pursuit of perfection, recognizing that their shared journey had profoundly shaped them.

Beyond her personal growth, Jammie found a new purpose in sharing her knowledge and experience. Mentoring younger riders, she found immense satisfaction in guiding and supporting them. Employing her personal triumphs and setbacks as teaching tools, she reminded them that equestrianism is not merely about technical perfection, but also about character development, resilience, and self-belief. She encouraged them to embrace challenges as opportunities for growth, learn from their mistakes, and find joy in pursuiting continuous learning. She instilled in them the importance of self-compassion, celebrating their achievements and learning from their setbacks with grace and maturity.

The lessons she imparted extended beyond the realm of dressage.

She emphasized the importance of balance and integrating their passions with other aspects of their lives, including academics, friendships, and family. She reminded them that success was not a destination but a continuous journey of growth, learning, and self-discovery. Her mentoring role fulfilled a deep-seated need to give back, to nurture the next generation of equestrians, and to share the wisdom she had gained through her own challenging yet rewarding journey.

The pressure to meet family expectations transformed. It was a source of pride, not a burden. She honored their history and dedication to the sport, but she also defined her path and interpretation of success. She recognized that genuine success wasn't about conforming to expectations, but about creating a definition that resonated with her values, passions, and vision for the future.

Jammie rediscovered simple life's joys. The quiet moments spent with Apollo, with the warm breath on her hand and the rhythmic sway of his gait as they walked along the trails, became sources of profound joy and contentment. Their shared connection transcended the arena; it was a bond of mutual trust, respect, and unwavering support. She learned to cherish these moments, appreciate the simple beauty of their companionship, and find solace and strength in their bond.

Once narrowly defined by pursuiting equestrian excellence, her life had expanded to encompass a rich tapestry of experiences, relationships, and pursuits. She achieved a fulfilling equilibrium, excelling as both a rider and a complete person. The Grand Prix victory was a significant achievement, a testament to her dedication and skill. However, it was the journey, the personal growth, and the newfound balance that truly represented her greatest triumph. It was a testament to her resilience, unwavering spirit, and ability to find fulfillment and joy in all aspects of her life. The stables' sunset filled the sky with orange and purple shades, reflecting Jammie's vibrant and harmonious life, where her heart beat in sync with Apollo's hooves, a life she had fully embraced. The Grand Prix marked a stage, yet her life progressed, increasingly prosperous and fulfilling.

Chapter 46: New Opportunities

The quiet satisfaction of a life lived fully settled over Jammie like a warm blanket. The Grand Prix victory, once a consuming obsession, now felt like a distant echo, a powerful memory that fueled her future rather than defining her present. She found herself drawn to new challenges, new opportunities that extended beyond the familiar confines of the dressage arena.

One such opportunity arose unexpectedly. Isabelle Werth's renowned dressage clinic was nearby. Initially, Jammie hesitated. Facing critique from this respected figure at the clinic rekindled past anxieties. The fear of judgment, of falling short, threatened to creep back in. But this time, the feeling was fleeting. She had learned to recognize these old demons and to greet them with a confident smile.

Jammie enrolled in the clinic, and a desire for continuous improvement and a thirst for knowledge that surpassed her desire for immediate recognition fueled her decision. The clinic was an incredible experience. Isabelle Werth's instruction was insightful, precise, and incredibly encouraging. She focused on technical corrections and the deeper connection between horse and rider, emphasizing the importance of communication, trust, and mutual respect. Jammie learned not only new techniques, but also a deeper understanding of her riding philosophy. She discovered subtle nuances in her communication with Apollo, refining her aids and deepening their partnership.

The other participants in the clinic were equally inspiring. There were seasoned professionals, young hopefuls, and everyone in between. The shared passion for dressage fostered camaraderie, creating a supportive environment where everyone was eager to learn and grow. Jammie discovered a new level of confidence, realizing she was not alone in her challenges and that even the most accomplished riders faced their doubts and insecurities. This realization was incredibly liberating. It freed her from the pressure of perfection, allowing her to embrace the journey of continuous learning.

Beyond the dressage clinic, Jammie explored other avenues of her passion. She volunteered to assist at a local therapeutic riding center, where she worked with children with disabilities. The experience was both humbling and enriching. Witnessing the transformative power of horses on these inexperienced riders, seeing the joy and confidence bloom in their eyes, touched Jammie deeply. The focus shifted from competition and personal achievement to something larger, something more meaningful. The work demanded patience, empathy, and a deep understanding of human interaction, which proved to be as valuable as her technical dressage skills.

She also started a blog, where she documents her experiences, shares her insights, and passes on her knowledge to a broader audience. She wrote about her training routines, successes and failures, thoughts on horsemanship, and reflections on the journey of becoming a dressage rider. It was a way to connect with fellow equestrians, to share her passion, and to contribute to the larger equestrian community. Refreshingly honest, vulnerable, and inspirational was her writing style. Her stories resonated with readers not only because of her equestrian expertise, but also because of her authenticity and willingness to share her struggles and triumphs. Her blog became a platform for fostering connections, creating a supportive community where riders of all levels could learn from one another, share their experiences, and inspire each other.

She continued to flourish academically. The discipline she had cultivated in dressage translated seamlessly into her studies. Excelling in her classes, she earned recognition for her academic achievements and equestrian prowess. Drawn to the world of equine science, she increasingly studied the biomechanics of movement, the physiology of the horse, and the intricate relationship between training methods and equine welfare. She realized that her passion for dressage extended beyond the aesthetic beauty of the movements; it encompassed a deeper understanding of the horse's physical and emotional well-being.

Her relationships continued to grow stronger. John's support remained unwavering, and his understanding of her ambitions was reassuring and inspiring. Their conversations now encompassed a wider range of topics, reflecting Jammie's expanding horizons. They explored future possibilities together, dreaming of shared adventures, both within and beyond the world of equestrianism. Their bond, forged in mutual respect and unwavering support, became the foundation for a bright and promising future.

The friendships she had cultivated also deepened, expanding beyond the immediate confines of the stable. She discovered a shared interest in art with one of her friends, embarking on collaborative projects that combined their talents and creativity. Another friend shared her passion for environmental conservation, and Jammie was involved in local initiatives to protect natural habitats and support sustainable practices. These friendships broadened her perspective, enriching her life with new experiences and deepening her understanding of the world beyond horses.

Jammie's relationship with Karen had evolved into a respectful professional collaboration. They continued to push each other, to learn from each other, and to celebrate each other's achievements.

A deep mutual respect, a testament to their shared passion for dressage and commitment to excellence, had replaced the rivalry that had once defined their relationship. They collaborated on training projects, sharing their expertise and insights, and creating a dynamic and mutually beneficial partnership.

Even her relationship with her family evolved. Her family's legacy, initially anxiety-inducing, now inspires pride. She honored her family's history while forging her path, creating her definition of success. She realized that genuine success was not about conforming to expectations, but about embracing her unique talents and passions, and living a life that resonated with her values and aspirations.

The rhythmic clop of Apollo's hooves on the ground, his warm breath on her cheek, and the shared moments of quiet understanding became the anchors of her life, symbols of the balance and fulfillment she had achieved. Jammie's life was a rich tapestry woven with threads of passion, resilience, and unwavering self-belief. The Grand Prix victory was a milestone, a testament to her dedication and skill. But it was the journey, the continuous growth, the embrace of new challenges, the deepening of her relationships, and pursuiting her passions that truly defined her story — a story that continued to unfold, vibrant, with every passing day. The future stretched before her, filled with possibilities as boundless as the sky above the stables. It was a future she embraced with open arms, ready to ride towards it with courage, grace, and unwavering determination.

Chapter 47: Strengthened Relationships

Jammie walked Apollo through the crisp morning air. The fall leaves swirled around her boots. Since the Grand Prix, the vibrant colors mirrored the richness and depth of her life had gained. The victory, once the pinnacle of her ambitions, now felt like a stepping stone — a testament to her capabilities that propelled her forward rather than anchoring her in place. Accomplishment, a warm glow beneath her skin, filled her, but this feeling blended with quiet contentment and a deep satisfaction in the journey itself.

Her relationship with John had reached a new level of intimacy and understanding. They weren't romantically involved. Recognizing her unwavering devotion to horses, he understood she was not a competitor but someone who deeply valued and admired her own exceptional talent and tireless dedication to the sport. She spent weekends on less-traveled trails. Jammie found his riding lessons endlessly amusing, his clumsy starts leading to too much laughter and support from her.

Their future, once a blurry horizon, now felt tangible, filled with the promise of shared dreams and mutual support. They discussed university, potential careers—John's interest in veterinary science aligning perfectly with Jammie's growing fascination with equine science—and building a life together, one where horses were not a part of their world but an integral part of its rhythm and harmony.

Her friendships also blossomed, extending beyond the confines of the stables and the dressage arena. Sarah, her artistic friend, had introduced Jammie to the world of equine portraiture. They spent hours together, Sarah meticulously sketching Apollo's elegant form. Jammie described the nuances of his movement, the subtle shifts in his posture and gait that revealed his emotions and intentions.

The resulting paintings were not artistic representations of a horse; they celebrated their unique bond, a testament to the deep connection between horse and rider. Their collaborative efforts culminated in an exhibition at a local gallery, showcasing their artistic talents and the elegance and grace of the horses they loved. The shared experience deepened their friendship, forging a bond that extended beyond their pursuits.

Meanwhile, Liam, her environmentally conscious friend, involved Jammie in a local project to restore a degraded meadow near the stables. They spent their weekends clearing invasive species, planting native wildflowers, and learning about the delicate balance of the ecosystem. The work was physically demanding, but deeply rewarding. Jammie discovered a newfound appreciation for the natural world, recognizing the interconnectedness of all living things and the importance of conservation efforts. She found a parallel between her meticulous care and attention to Apollo's well-being and the need to protect the fragile environment where he thrived. The shared cause provided a purpose that extended beyond her ambitions, offering fulfillment that resonated deeply within her.

What was most unexpected was the transformation in her relationship with Karen. The fierce rivalry that had once defined their interactions had given way to a grudging respect, a hesitant friendship, and genuine collaboration. They realized their shared passion for dressage transcended personal differences, forming a foundation for mutual understanding and appreciation. They began training together, pushing each other's limits, offering constructive criticism, and celebrating each other's successes.

Karen's sharp eye for detail and her methodical approach complemented Jammie's intuitive connection with her horse, creating a cooperation that elevated their riding. They started a joint training program, assisting younger riders and mentoring them with the patience and wisdom gained from their shared experiences. This unexpected partnership enhanced their riding and enriched their lives, proving that competition wasn't about defeating an opponent, but about constantly striving for improvement.

Even her relationship with her family had undergone a subtle shift. The constant pressure to live up to her family's illustrious equestrian legacy had eased, giving way to a sense of pride and mutual respect. Her parents, initially focused on her competitive achievements, now celebrated her holistic approach to horsemanship, her commitment to ethical training practices, her involvement in community projects, and her growing interest in equine science. They had learned to appreciate her individuality, her unique path toward excellence, and her ability to forge her destiny. Family dinners were no longer tense occasions dominated by performance anxieties, but relaxed gatherings filled with laughter, shared stories, and genuine affection.

One crisp evening, as the sun dipped below the horizon, casting long shadows across the stable yard, Jammie sat beside John, Apollo's warm breath gently ruffled her hair. The rhythmic clinking of his bridle and the soft sigh of the wind through the trees created a symphony of peace and contentment. She realized her journey had not merely been about achieving a Grand Prix victory but about discovering herself, forging meaningful relationships, embracing new challenges, and creating a life infused with passion, resilience, and unwavering self-belief. She had ridden through storms and emerged stronger, wiser, and more deeply connected to her world, her horses, and the people who loved her.

No longer fearing the future, she embraced its promise of growth, support, and potential, riding towards it with grace, courage, and determination. A long, winding path lay ahead, yet she was ready, her strongest relationships her steadfast companions on this extraordinary adventure. As Apollo's hooves rhythmically beat on the stable floor, mirroring the steady beat of her hopeful, joyful heart, a quiet satisfaction filled her, reflecting a life well-lived.

Chapter 48: Personal Growth

The quiet contentment that settled over Jammie's life after the Grand Prix wasn't a passive state; it was a vibrant blossoming. It wasn't the absence of challenges, but a newfound resilience in facing them. The anxieties that had once consumed her — the crippling fear of failure — had retreated, replaced by a quiet confidence that hummed beneath her skin, a steady pulse of self-belief. This wasn't a sudden transformation, a miraculous overnight shift, but a gradual unfolding, a slow and steady growth that mirrored the meticulous training of a dressage horse.

One of the most significant changes was her approach to training Apollo. Previously, external expectations fueled her training; she strived for perfection. Now her focus had shifted. Observing Apollo's subtle cues and the nuances of his responses, she listened more intently. Recognizing his emotional state, she adjusted her training accordingly. She introduced elements of liberty training, allowing Apollo to express himself freely, fostering a deeper bond of trust and understanding between them. She discovered a joy in the simple act of communicating with him, a silent conversation woven through the intricate movements of their partnership.

This shift in approach extended beyond her relationship with Apollo. Mentoring younger riders at the stables, she shared her knowledge and experience with a patience and empathy that surprised even herself. She not only helped them with the technical aspects of dressage but also the mental and emotional challenges of competition. The importance of self-belief, the resilience to overcome setbacks, and the profound connection between horse and rider were lessons she taught them. She found deep satisfaction in nurturing the talents of others, in helping them discover their own potential — a fulfillment that resonated far beyond the thrill of personal victory.

Her academic pursuits also took a significant turn. The fascination with equine science that had sparked during her preparation for the Grand Prix now blazed. Devoting herself to her studies, she devoured books on equine anatomy, physiology, and biomechanics. She began researching the latest advancements in equine health and welfare, eager to integrate this knowledge into her training methods. She even started a small project, analyzing the impact of various training techniques on a horse's musculoskeletal system, using motion-capture technology to measure subtle movements and pinpoint areas for improvement. This pursuit was more than an academic exercise; it reflected her deepening commitment to her horse's well-being and desire to contribute to the field of equine science.

Her newfound confidence also extended to her social life. She blossomed in her relationship with John, their connection deepening with each shared experience. They didn't ride together; instead, they explored their shared interests by planning trips to equine research centers and attending lectures on animal welfare. From groundbreaking science to the ethical considerations of equestrian sports, their talks encompassed a wide range of topics. Their mutual respect and understanding created a secure and supportive environment where they could flourish. Their shared passion for horses had cemented their bond, transcending the typical teenage romance and laying the foundation for a lifelong partnership.

Even her relationship with her family evolved, moving beyond the pressure-cooker atmosphere that had characterized her teenage years. Her parents, witnessing her holistic approach to horsemanship and her dedication to personal growth, finally understood that competition victories did not define her success solely. They were proud of her commitment to ethical training practices, her involvement in community projects, and her burgeoning academic achievements. Family dinners became occasions for genuine connection and shared laughter, replacing the tension of previous years. Her siblings also found a renewed appreciation for her, seeing beyond her competitive spirit and acknowledging her growing maturity and unwavering self-belief.

Her friendship with Sarah continued to flourish. Their collaborative art project led to several more exhibitions, showcasing the beauty of the horses and the power of creative collaboration.

Sarah's artistic talent added an extra dimension to Jammie's understanding of horses. Through the strokes of her brush, she revealed the subtleties of their emotional states. Their friendship, built on mutual respect and a shared passion, became a constant source of inspiration and support.

Jammie's involvement with Liam and the meadow restoration project expanded. Their commitment to environmental conservation evolved into a shared passion, extending beyond the small meadow to encompass broader community engagement. They organized workshops on sustainable land management, educating others about preserving natural habitats. Jammie's work with the project taught her the value of teamwork and collaborative effort towards a larger cause, demonstrating that her self-discovery extended beyond her achievements and into environmental advocacy. The project's success fueled her desire to become a voice for environmental conservation within the equestrian community, promoting ethical practices that respected the welfare of both horses and their environment.

The transformation in Jammie's relationship with Karen was equally profound. Their shared passion for dressage became a source of mutual support and inspiration. They continued to push and challenge each other, but their rivalry had evolved into a healthy competition, a collaboration aimed at mutual improvement.

They judged younger riders together, and their shared experience and expertise created a synergistic and insightful partnership. Their collaboration on training programs proved invaluable, helping them to fine-tune their methods and mentor the next generation of equestrians with wisdom and patience.

The winter months brought new challenges and opportunities. The long hours spent meticulously caring for Apollo in the stables allowed Jammie to develop a deeper understanding of his needs and sensitivities. She experimented with new training techniques, integrating elements of classical dressage with modern approaches. She observed the subtle shifts in Apollo's moods and responses, constantly adjusting her methods to ensure his comfort and well-being. The cold weather provided an opportunity to focus on indoor training, developing precision and harmony within the arena's confines.

As spring arrived, bringing the promise of new beginnings, Jammie felt a surge of excitement and anticipation. She entered several local competitions, not driven by the pressure to win, but by the desire to test her skills, to refine her technique, and to enjoy the process. She approached each competition with a calm confidence, focusing on her connection with Apollo and the pleasure of their shared journey. The victories were sweet, but the valid reward lay in their partnership's continual growth and refinement. The insecure teenager entering the Grand Prix was far removed from the woman she'd become. Now, she rode with a quiet strength, a profound understanding of herself and her horse, and a passionate commitment to a life enriched by the grace and elegance of dressage. The journey was far from over, but she rode towards the future, confident of her abilities, ready to face whatever challenges may lie ahead, with courage, grace, and unwavering self-belief. Atop her magnificent horse, the future held endless possibilities, and Jammie was ready to embrace them all.

Chapter 49: Future Goals

The summer sun warmed Jammie's face as she sat astride Apollo, the familiar scent of hay and leather filling her senses. Her life irrevocably shifted after the Grand Prix, a pivotal moment now seeming distant. She wasn't a dressage rider anymore; she was a burgeoning equestrian scientist, a mentor, an environmental advocate, and a young woman brimming with confidence and purpose. Once a hazy landscape of anxieties and uncertainties, the future now stretched before her, a vibrant tapestry woven with ambition and possibility.

Her immediate goal was to secure a scholarship to the prestigious University of California, Davis, renowned for its exceptional equine science program. This wasn't simply a desire for academic advancement but a strategic move to solidify her future in equine care and research. She spent hours poring over application forms, meticulously crafting essays showcasing her academic prowess and unwavering commitment to horses' well-being. She detailed her independent research project on the impact of training techniques on equine musculoskeletal systems, highlighting her innovative use of motion-capture technology and her dedication to scientific rigor.

Included were glowing recommendations from her professors and mentors and testimonials underscoring her dedication, intelligence, and exceptional work ethic. The application process was challenging, demanding precision, attention to detail, and a meticulous approach, which mirrored her dressage training. Yet, unlike the nerve-wracking pressure of competition, this challenge felt invigorating, empowering, and fulfilling.

Beyond academics, Jammie aimed to establish herself as a respected figure in the local equestrian community. To help riders with all skill levels, she intended to expand her mentoring program and create a structured curriculum. Workshops blending technical and mental training, providing new riders with life skills and competition preparation, were her vision. Instilling resilience and self-belief: Her goal was to instill in them the same resilience and self-belief which had marked her transformation. She envisioned a space where young riders could learn the intricacies of dressage while developing a deep and meaningful connection with their equine partners, fostering ethical and sustainable horsemanship practices. She sought to create a supportive environment where collaboration thrived, one in which camaraderie and mutual respect among riders enhanced the overall experience, enriching their passion for the sport and their love of horses.

Jammie's commitment to environmental conservation continued to grow. The meadow restoration project: She planned to expand it, transforming the project into a model for sustainable land management in the wider community. She hoped to secure funding for larger-scale initiatives that involved local schools and community organizations in the effort. She envisioned workshops and educational programs to raise awareness about the ecological importance of preserving natural habitats. Her long-term vision encompassed promoting environmentally friendly practices within the equestrian community, advocating for sustainable barn management, promoting responsible waste disposal methods, and encouraging riders to make conscious choices that minimize their environmental impact. This wasn't about preserving meadows; it was about fostering a deep and abiding respect for the environment that intertwined seamlessly with her love for horses and equestrian sports.

Her artistic collaboration with Sarah continued to thrive. They planned a larger exhibition, showcasing their work to a broader audience and potentially securing gallery representation. Jammie's vision extended beyond simple displays of equine beauty; she wanted to convey the essence of the horse, the emotional depths, the silent communication, the symbiotic relationship between horse and rider. Sarah's artistic talent would translate these subtleties onto canvas, creating pieces that resonate emotionally with viewers, evoking wonder and admiration for these magnificent creatures. The collaboration would further strengthen their friendship, creating a powerful partnership that fueled their artistic growth. The shared passion for horses, their profound respect for the animals, and their ability to communicate their message artistically would be the cornerstone of their continued success.

Jammie's relationship with Apollo continued to evolve. Her dedication extended beyond competitions and training; it encompassed a holistic approach to his well-being. To ensure optimal nutrition, she meticulously monitored his diet. She meticulously documented his training progress, analyzing his strengths and weaknesses, and adjusting her training methods to optimize his performance and comfort. She integrated alternative therapies, such as acupuncture and massage, to address any minor ailments, ensuring he remained in peak condition. Their bond grew deeper, a silent understanding forged through years of shared experiences, a testament to their unwavering trust and mutual respect. She knew his well-being was essential to her success, and she absolutely committed to his health and happiness.

Her personal life also flourished. Her relationship with John strengthened their shared passion for horses, forming the bedrock of a solid and supportive partnership. They planned weekend getaways to equestrian centers and research facilities, immersing themselves in equine science and conservation. Philosophical discussions about animal welfare and the ethics of equestrian sports characterized their conversations, moving beyond surface-level chatter. Because of their shared intellectual curiosity and mutual respect, they experienced significant intellectual growth, strengthening their bond and commitment. Their unwavering support for each other's individual goals and aspirations enriched their personal and professional lives. Their future together was bright, filled with possibilities and shared adventures.

The future brimmed with potential. Jammie was carving her path with unwavering determination. She envisioned herself not just as a successful dressage rider, but as a leader in the equestrian world, a respected voice in equine science and a passionate advocate for environmental conservation.

Challenges and setbacks had marked her journey, but precisely those hurdles shaped her character and fueled her determination. She had learned the value of resilience, the importance of self-belief, and the power of perseverance. The Grand Prix victory wasn't simply a triumph in competition; it was a testament to her personal growth, a turning point that propelled her towards a future brimming with endless possibilities. The insecure teen had become a self-assured, successful young woman; her journey continued. The future stretched before her, a boundless canvas upon which she would paint her dreams, aspirations, and unwavering commitment to a life intertwined with the elegance and grace of the equestrian world.

Chapter 50: A Sense of Accomplishment

As Jammie approached Apollo, the crisp fall air chilled her cheeks; the steady beat of his hooves soothed the turmoil inside her. As if a lifetime had passed, the memory of the Grand Prix felt distant, yet its powerful influence, the way it had acted as a catalyst for change in her life, remained palpable. While not achieved within the confines of a traditional arena, her victory was a resounding and profound validation of her unwavering dedication, persistent perseverance, and unshakeable belief in her own capabilities. Her success stood as a powerful testament, showcasing not only the countless hours of diligent practice and skill-honing but also highlighting the personal sacrifices she endured and the unwavering support system that surrounded and championed her throughout her journey. Her profound accomplishment yielded a quiet satisfaction, exceeding the competition's fleeting glory.

This wasn't merely the satisfaction of winning; it was a deeper understanding of her potential. Grand Prix pressure, expectation, failure, fear: formidable foes. Yet, by confronting them head-on and pushing herself beyond her perceived limits, Jammie discovered a strength and resilience she hadn't known she possessed. The fear hadn't vanished entirely; it was now a familiar companion, a shadow she could acknowledge and manage, rather than a force that paralyzed her. This newfound self-awareness was perhaps the most significant reward of her journey.

The blustery November day delivered the tangible reward of her hard work—an acceptance letter from UC Davis, a moment she'd long awaited. The announcement, "Congratulations, Ms. Jammie," echoed the thrilling fanfare of her Grand Prix win. This substantial scholarship celebrated her academic achievements, her passion for equine science, and secured her future career in the field. The prestigious reputation of the university meant nothing to them; however, the dream of attending belonged to her alone.

Word spread quickly among the local equestrian community, attracting inexperienced riders eager to learn from her experience and wisdom. Her workshops were a blend of technical instruction and mental conditioning, empowering riders to develop their equestrian skills, self-confidence, and resilience. She emphasized the importance of building a strong bond with their horses, fostering ethical and sustainable horsemanship practices. The program became a vibrant hub of shared passion, mutual support, and collaborative growth, reflecting Jammie's commitment to nurturing the next generation of equestrian athletes and advocates. She found immense satisfaction in witnessing her students' progress, in their burgeoning self-assurance and love for the sport. Their successes became her own, a testament to the transformative power of mentorship and the joy of sharing her passion.

The meadow restoration project also gained momentum. Local schools and community groups joined forces, turning the initial initiative into a larger-scale environmental conservation effort.

Jammie secured grant funding, enabling her to implement innovative, sustainable land management practices. She organized workshops and educational programs that raised awareness about the environmental importance of preserving natural habitats. She even partnered with a local organic farm to use sustainably harvested hay for her horses and those taking part in her mentoring program, creating a closed-loop system that highlights the interdependence between ecological health and equestrian practices. This holistic approach enabled her seamless integration of her passion for horses with her commitment to environmental stewardship, creating a powerful and meaningful legacy.

The art exhibition with Sarah was a resounding success. Their collaborative artwork, a series of evocative pieces depicting the powerful bond between humans and horses, resonated deeply with viewers. The exhibition showcased their artistic talents and conveyed a profound message about animal welfare, ethical horsemanship, and the profound connection between horses and riders. The critical acclaim they received validated their artistic vision and their commitment to using their art to inspire and educate. It was a momentous achievement, a culmination of years of creative collaboration, and a testament to the power of their shared passion. The financial success allowed them to continue their work, taking on larger projects and broadening their reach to new audiences.

Beyond the competition, Jammie and Apollo developed a deeper bond. Their relationship went beyond a typical rider-horse bond, growing into deep mutual respect and understanding. Maintaining a vigilant watch over his health, she continuously ensured his well-being remained her utmost concern and priority. Through their daily routines, encompassing everything from intensive training sessions to the peaceful moments spent in quiet grooming, they developed a connection that was deeper and more meaningful than any spoken words, a silent understanding built upon years of shared experiences. She realized the wrong horse, not Apollo, was her assigned partner. He surpassed the limitations of being just a horse;

Her relationship with John also flourished. Their shared passion for horses and commitment to environmental stewardship cemented their bond. They embarked on many adventures together, exploring new equestrian centers, attending conferences on equine science, and volunteering at wildlife sanctuaries. Their conversations ranged from the complexities of dressage movements to the ethical implications of modern agricultural practices, demonstrating a shared intellectual curiosity and a deep commitment to shared goals. Their mutual support and unwavering belief in each other strengthened their relationship, creating a solid foundation for a future built on shared passions and mutual respect.

Individual achievements did not fully encompass the sense of accomplishment; Jammie's transformation wasn't simply about winning competitions or achieving academic success; it was about developing resilience, self-belief, and an unwavering pursuit of her dreams. The Grand Prix victory had been a pivotal moment. Still, the accurate measure of her success lay in her ability to navigate challenges, overcome obstacles, and emerge stronger and more confident. The journey had taught her the importance of perseverance, hard work, and the significance of believing in herself, even when faced with overwhelming odds. Triumphs, regardless of scale, formed a narrative of progress and strength.

Jammie's journey, she realized, had only just begun. The future held endless possibilities, each one a testament to the dedication, perseverance, and hard work that had shaped her life. Her success was not a personal achievement, but a testament to the transformative power of passion, resilience, and the enduring bond between humans and horses. It fully embodied a life well-lived, a testament to pursuing excellence, symbolizing limitless potential for those daring to dream. The future, bright and brimming with potential, beckoned her forward, and with Apollo at her side, she was ready to ride into it with unwavering courage and boundless enthusiasm. The feeling wasn't of accomplishment, but of anticipation for the future.

Chapter 51: Looking Ahead

The California sun warmed Jammie's face as she sat on the porch of her family's ranch, Apollo grazing peacefully in the nearby paddock. The scent of eucalyptus and damp earth filled the air, a familiar comfort after the whirlwind of the past year. Looking out at the rolling hills, the vibrant green of the newly restored meadow — a testament to her efforts — settled a profound sense of peace within her. The Grand Prix felt like a lifetime ago, yet its impact reverberated through every fiber of her being. It wasn't the victory, but the transformation it sparked within her.

She felt like a distant memory, the insecure, self-doubting teenager she once was. The pressure to live up to her family's legacy, the constant comparisons to Karen, the crippling fear of failure—these had once defined her, shaping her every move. But the Grand Prix had become a crucible, forging a strength and resilience she hadn't known she possessed. The victory was a symbol, a tangible representation of her hard work, dedication, and unwavering self-belief. More importantly, it catalyzed a more profound self-discovery, self-acceptance, and personal growth that continued to unfold.

Her academic pursuits at the University of California, Davis, were thriving. Challenging and exhilarating, the rigorous coursework in equine science pushed her intellectual boundaries. The camaraderie among her classmates, shared late-night study sessions fueled by copious amounts of coffee and a common passion, fostered a belonging she hadn't expected. The research opportunities, access to innovative technology, and the mentorship of leading experts in the field opened doors she hadn't even dreamed of. She contributed to groundbreaking research on equine health and welfare, her work blending scientific inquiry and her deep-seated love for horses.

The mentoring program, once a tentative venture, had blossomed into a thriving initiative. She found immense satisfaction in guiding younger riders, witnessing their growth and development, not in the arena, but also in their personal lives. The focus wasn't solely on technical skills but on nurturing self-confidence, fostering resilience, and emphasizing the importance of ethical and sustainable horsemanship practices. She watched as her students, initially shy, transformed into confident, capable riders, their faces alight with passion and self-belief. The success of her program not only fueled her love for her work, but also reinforced the profound and positive impact she could have on the lives of others, inspiring her to continue her important work.

The meadow restoration project, initially conceived as a modest undertaking, continued to flourish and expand far beyond its original parameters. Working with local schools and community groups built a strong sense of shared responsibility for environmental stewardship. New grant money let her implement innovative sustainable land management and expand educational outreach to more people. The project became a living testament to the power of community involvement, the importance of environmental conservation, and the intertwined nature of human and ecological well-being. The sustainable hay production, now supplying many stables in the region, provided a practical demonstration of environmentally friendly practices in the equestrian world.

Her artistic collaboration with Sarah continued to evolve. Their joint exhibitions, which now traveled to galleries across the state, captured the imagination of both art enthusiasts and horse lovers.

Their evocative portrayals of the profound connection between humans and horses resonated deeply, sparking conversations about animal welfare, ethical horsemanship, and the importance of respecting and celebrating the natural world. The critical acclaim and financial success allowed them to pursue larger-scale projects, collaborate with other artists, and expand their artistic vision.

Jammie's relationship with Apollo remained the cornerstone of her life. Their bond transcended the rider-horse dynamic, a testament to years of mutual respect, understanding, and unwavering loyalty.

Their daily interactions, from training sessions to quiet grooming moments, were a constant source of comfort and joy. Apollo's presence grounded her, reminding her of the unwavering support she could always count on, a testament to their unique bond. He remained an integral part of her life, her confidante, her partner, and her friend.

Her relationship with John also deepened their shared values and passions, strengthening their connection. Their lives intertwined seamlessly, their mutual support and unwavering belief in each other, forming a solid foundation for their future. They embarked on recent adventures, exploring new equestrian centers, attending conferences, and continuing their volunteer work at wildlife sanctuaries. Their discussions, as always, covered a wide range of topics, from the subtleties of dressage movements to the broader implications of sustainable agriculture; their shared intellect and common goals strengthened their bond.

The years ahead stretched before her, brimming with possibilities. She overcame the challenges, pressure, self-doubt, and fear, forging a resilience that empowers her to face any future obstacles. She knew that self-discovery was an ongoing, continuous process of growth and evolution. But she approached the future with quiet confidence, deep self-awareness, and an unwavering belief in her capabilities.

She had achieved so much: a Grand Prix victory, a prestigious scholarship, a flourishing mentoring program, a successful art career, and a thriving environmental conservation project. Yet the accurate measure of her success wasn't in these individual accomplishments. Still, in the person she had become—a confident, compassionate, and resilient young woman who had harnessed her passion for horses to create a meaningful and fulfilling life. The future beckoned, a tapestry woven with ambition, opportunity, and the unwavering support of those she loved. She embraced it with open arms, ready to ride into the unknown with steadfast courage and boundless enthusiasm. Apollo's gentle whinny reassured her; she wasn't alone, her loyal companion entering the future with her. The future was hers to shape, a thrilling prospect filled with the promise of recent adventures and continued personal and professional growth. The challenging journey, requiring sacrifice and perseverance, yielded unparalleled rewards, exceeding all expectations. And that, she knew, was the beginning.

Chapter 52: Lasting Impact

The quiet hum of the ranch, which had once underscored her anxieties, now lulled her with a comforting sound, a peaceful counterpoint to her former worries. As Apollo breathed rhythmically in his nearby stall, the steady sound was a constant source of comfort and reassurance. Competing in the Grand Prix, a high-stakes event, established her in the dressage world and shifted the direction of her life.

A quiet confidence now filled her life, having replaced her former persistent self-doubt. No longer did the fear of failing to live up to her family's esteemed legacy and the persistent anxiety that gnawed at her hold any sway over her. Despite the excitement and success of the Grand Prix, those underlying insecurities had not vanished like magic. Through experience, she came to understand that setbacks, far from being defeats, served as significant learning experiences; each misstep became a stepping stone in her ongoing journey of personal and professional growth. Overcoming challenges gave depth and perspective on her accomplishments.

Her academic pursuits at the University of California, Davis, continued to flourish. She excelled in her equine science courses, embracing the intellectual rigor with an unwavering enthusiasm. Once fueled by caffeine and anxiety, the late-night study sessions were now punctuated by laughter and shared dreams, forged in the crucible of shared challenges. Her research on equine biomechanics, a project that combined her passion for horses with her scientific curiosity, was progressing rapidly, gaining recognition from leading researchers. She even secured a coveted summer internship at a prestigious equine research facility in Kentucky, an opportunity that would allow her to work alongside world-renowned experts and contribute to groundbreaking studies in equine health and welfare.

The mentoring program she started had evolved into a fully fledged initiative, nurturing inexperienced riders, not in their technical skills, but also their emotional and mental fortitude. She developed a unique curriculum that combines rigorous training with mindfulness, resilience, and ethical horsemanship lessons. She witnessed firsthand the transformative power of her program, watching her students blossom into confident, capable riders, their self-belief shining through in their performances. The success of her program fueled her passion, reinforcing her belief in the power of mentorship and the profound impact she could have on the lives of young equestrians.

The meadow restoration project, born from a simple desire to reclaim a neglected corner of the ranch, had become a symbol of community engagement and environmental stewardship. It had grown beyond its initial scope, encompassing a network of schools, community organizations, and local businesses working together towards a common goal. She secured funding for expanded research into sustainable land management practices within equestrian environments, starting trials on reduced tillage techniques and native plant regeneration. The project became a showcase for responsible environmental stewardship, demonstrating how the equestrian world could minimize its ecological footprint while enhancing biodiversity and the well-being of the surrounding environment. Ecosystem. The sustainable hay production, now supplying stables throughout the region, offered a tangible example of environmentally conscious practice.

Her artistic collaborations with Sarah continued to flourish, their paintings and sculptures capturing the essence of the human-animal bond and the majestic beauty of horses. Their exhibitions, attracting increasing attention from art critics and collectors, generated meaningful discussions about the ethical treatment of animals and the interconnectedness of humans and the natural world. They secured commissions for large-scale public art installations, which provided a platform for their message of environmental responsibility and compassion towards animals to reach a wider audience. Their success enabled them to expand their art projects on a larger scale, embracing new media and challenging artistic boundaries; their collaboration flourished as their art evolved.

Jammie's relationship with Apollo deepened their bond, a testament to the years of unwavering loyalty and mutual respect. Their daily interactions, filled with quiet moments of grooming and training sessions, remained a source of immense joy and comfort. Apollo's presence in her life was a constant reassurance, a reminder of the steadfast support and unwavering companionship she could always rely on. He remained her confidante, her partner, her friend.

Her relationship with John had also blossomed. Their shared values, mutual support, and common passions solidified their bond. Their adventures together, exploring new equestrian centers and attending conferences, continued to enrich their lives. They volunteered together at wildlife sanctuaries, combining their passion for animals with their commitment to conservation. Their shared intellect and unwavering belief in each other strengthened their foundation, fostering a relationship built on mutual understanding, trust, and love. Shared experiences and laughter marked their journeys together, whether on horseback or otherwise, strengthening their bond with each passing day.

Looking towards the future, Jammie felt profound gratitude and quiet anticipation. The challenges she had faced and the setbacks she had overcome had shaped her into a stronger, more resilient, and self-aware individual. The Grand Prix victory had been a pivotal moment, a turning point in her life, but the journey, personal growth, and lessons learned along the way truly defined her success. She embraced the future with open arms, ready to face whatever challenges lay ahead, armed with the confidence, resilience, and compassion she had cultivated along her path.

She knew that her journey of self-discovery was an ongoing process, a continuous evolution. Still, she approached the future with unwavering courage, quiet confidence, and the unwavering support of her family, friends, and her beloved Apollo. The future, she realized, was a breathtaking canvas, waiting to be painted with the vibrant hues of her passions and dreams. Loyal companion present, she rode toward the unknown.

Chapter 53: Continued Passion

As Jammie guided Apollo through the early morning mist, the crisp fall air nipped at her cheeks. A comforting aroma of damp earth and pine needles filled her lungs, grounding her in the present. The Grand Prix felt like a lifetime ago, a distant memory yet vividly etched in her mind. The victory, accolades, and celebrations were all wonderful and exhilarating, but what truly resonated was the profound sense of accomplishment — the quiet satisfaction of having overcome her deepest fears. It wasn't about winning; it was about the journey, the relentless pursuit of excellence, the unwavering dedication to her craft.

Her days were a tapestry woven with threads of passion and purpose. Dressage remained at the heart of her life, but it was no longer the sole defining factor of her life. A newfound balance had tempered the intense focus and relentless pursuit of perfection, a perspective she hadn't possessed before. Her training sessions with Apollo were less about achieving flawless performances and more about nurturing their deep connection, savoring the shared moments of understanding and trust that blossomed between them. The elegance of their movements, the effortless grace of their partnership, was a testament to their evolving bond, a symphony of movement that transcended the boundaries of competition.

She continued to compete, of course. The thrill of the arena, the electric energy of the crowd, and the exhilarating challenge of pushing herself and her horse to their limits were still potent draws.

But her approach had changed. A healthy ambition had replaced the overwhelming pressure to succeed—a desire to improve, refine her skills, and explore the ever-evolving nuances of dressage constantly. With calm confidence, she approached each competition, prioritizing the process over outcome and valuing the journey as much as the destination. She found joy in the quiet moments of connection with Apollo, in the shared breaths and the mutual understanding that passed between them without words.

At the University of California, Davis, she found continued challenge and inspiration in her studies. Though initially intimidating, studying equine biomechanics ultimately proved incredibly rewarding. Through countless hours of data analysis and in-depth study of research papers, her passion for understanding the complex mechanics of equine locomotion deepened and solidified. My summer internship in Kentucky proved to be a transformative experience, offering invaluable hands-on experience as I collaborated with leading researchers within the field, significantly enhancing my professional skills and knowledge. Her contributions to significant equine health and welfare studies appeared in prestigious scientific journals. This academic success improved her equestrian skills by providing a better understanding of the physical and physiological demands on horses during intense training and competition.

The mentoring program thrived, becoming a beacon for inexperienced riders seeking guidance and support. Jammie's unique curriculum, combining rigorous training with mindfulness and resilience exercises, helped students develop their riding skills, mental fortitude, and emotional intelligence. She witnessed firsthand the transformative power of her program, watching shy and insecure inexperienced riders blossom into confident and capable equestrians. Their achievements reflected her own, showcasing her work's effect and mentorship's importance within equestrian sports. She expanded the program, offering workshops and online resources to reach a wider audience, creating a community of support and shared passion.

The meadow restoration project continued to blossom, broadening its reach and effect. Initially a modest experiment, the sustainable hay production initiative has dramatically evolved, achieving remarkable success as a thriving business venture providing eco-conscious hay to many stables across the broader regional area. Regional and national awards recognized the project's innovative sustainable land management in equestrian areas. Jammie's efforts in reducing tillage and boosting native plant life earned praise from top environmental groups. She secured further funding for expanded research, starting studies on the impact of different grazing practices on soil health and biodiversity. The project became a model for sustainable land management within the equestrian world, showcasing the potential for positive environmental impact within the equestrian community.

Her artistic partnership with Sarah continued to thrive. Each year, their exhibitions attracted more visitors, earning both critical praise and significant public attention. Their art depicted a deep love for horses and a firm commitment to animal welfare. Through large-scale public art, they made powerful statements about humanity's relationship with nature, igniting discussions on animal ethics and environmental stewardship. Nationally acclaimed, their work earned them many awards and elevated their status in the art world. Encouraged by positive feedback, they resolved to leverage their art for sustainability and animal welfare.

Jammie's relationship with Apollo remained her sanctuary, a steadfast source of comfort and companionship. Their daily routines, the silent understanding that flowed between them, and the mutual respect and unwavering loyalty formed the bedrock of their bond. Apollo was more than a horse; he was family, a constant source of strength and unwavering support. They cherished their shared moments as treasures, reminding them of their unbreakable connection. Apollo's gentle demeanor and unwavering presence were a constant source of calm amidst the ever-changing tide of life's events.

Her relationship with John thrived, growing stronger with each passing year. Their shared passions, their mutual support, their shared adventures—these solidified their bond. Their shared love of animals and the environment fueled their collaboration on multiple conservation projects. They'd built a balanced life—successful careers alongside strong relationships. Mutual support of their dreams built trust and understanding, strengthening their connection. They grew and supported each other throughout their life together.

As time went on, year after year, Jammie persistently pursued her passion for riding, consistently engaging in training and competitive events. The significance of the ribbons and trophies, however, had diminished. She had discovered not only her voice but also her sense of purpose and the direction her life took.

Her life exemplified perseverance, self-belief, and passionate dedication. The Grand Prix victory had been a pivotal milestone on her journey. Still, her continuous growth, tireless dedication, and steadfast commitment to self-discovery truly defined her enduring success. She knew that her journey of self-discovery was an ongoing process, a perpetual evolution, and she was ready to embrace the future, one ride at a time. The canvas of her future lay before her, a vast expanse waiting to be filled with vibrant colors and bold strokes, her unwavering passion guiding her every step. And with Apollo, her loyal companion, by her side, she confidently rode into the unknown, ready to embrace whatever the future might bring.

Chapter 54: Themes of the Story

As the sun descended past the horizon, extended shadows stretched across the vast Kentucky landscape. Jammie, on the porch of her recently constructed farmhouse, observed the vibrant colors illuminating the sky, which served as a perfect visual complement to the sense of peaceful reflection that had enveloped her. The cherished narrative of the Grand Prix followed the passage of time, and each segment enriched it with a unique blend of obstacles, victories, and important personal growth. In retrospect, the victory seemed to take a backseat to the journey that it symbolized and represented. They did not emphasize getting awards, enthusiastic cheers, or showing capability.

The pressure to live up to her family's equestrian legacy had once felt like an insurmountable weight, a constant, nagging voice whispering doubts and insecurities. In her younger years, she had spent so much time striving for external validation and chasing perfection in the arena, perpetually falling short of her own impossibly high standards. With its intense pressure and fierce competition, the Grand Prix had become a catalyst for profound self-reflection. It forced her to confront her vulnerabilities, to acknowledge her fears, and ultimately to embrace the imperfections that made her unique herself. The victory wasn't a testament to flawlessness but to resilience, to the courage to rise above self-doubt and to persevere despite the odds.

The years that followed were a testament to her developing understanding of balance. Dressage, her lifelong passion, remained a central part of her life, but it was no longer the sole focus. She had learned to savor the quiet moments of connection with Apollo, appreciating the subtle nuances of their partnership and the artistry of their movements, which transcended the confines of competition. She discovered the joy of teaching, mentoring inexperienced riders, sharing her passion, and guiding them on their journeys of self-discovery.

Her program, a unique blend of technical instruction and mindfulness practices, empowered her students to develop their skills, emotional resilience, and mental strength. Watching them blossom, confident and capable, fueled her sense of purpose, a deeper satisfaction than any individual achievement could offer.

Her academic pursuits, initially a means to an end, had blossomed into a rewarding intellectual endeavor. Research in equine biomechanics offered a profound understanding of movement's intricate mechanics, deepening her appreciation for the complex partnership between horse and rider. Her work in sustainable land management, driven by a growing commitment to environmental stewardship, had extended far beyond her stables, affecting the broader equestrian community and fostering a more sustainable approach to the sport. The meadow restoration project, a testament to her vision and unwavering commitment, now serves as a model for environmentally conscious equestrian practices. It wasn't merely about restoring land, but creating a model for sustainable equestrianism that would benefit both horses and the planet.

Her art, a collaborative venture with Sarah, had become a powerful vehicle for social change. Drawing on increasingly larger crowds, their exhibitions served as platforms to promote animal welfare and raise awareness about environmental issues. The potent imagery, showing the spirit and grace of horses, prompted discussions, altered viewpoints, and motivated action. While their recognition was rewarding, their primary goal stayed the same—to use art to promote a more ethical and sustainable future. Their work affected the community, sparking conversations about environmentalism that transcended art.

Her relationship with John had blossomed into a deep and enduring partnership, built on shared passions and unwavering mutual support. They navigated life's challenges together, their bond strengthened by their shared commitment to conservation and their dedication to making a positive impact on the world. They had created a life rich in purpose, a testament to the power of shared values and mutual support. Their journey together was a beautiful tapestry woven with threads of shared dreams, unwavering support, and mutual growth. Their successes were not merely individual accomplishments; they were collaborative efforts, a testament to the power of partnership.

Looking at the darkening sky, Jammie felt a deep gratitude. The Grand Prix victory had been a significant milestone. Still, the journey-the unwavering pursuit of personal growth, the commitment to her passions, and the enduring relationships she cultivated along the way—had truly shaped her life. Self-doubt had once consumed the young, insecure girl, but she transformed into a confident, compassionate woman driven by a deep sense of purpose and an unwavering belief in her potential. She learned that genuine success comes not only from external validation or material achievements, but from rich experiences, deep relationships, and positive impact on the world.

The lessons leaned in the saddle transcended the arena, shaping her perspective on life. She had discovered that resilience, perseverance, and self-belief were essential ingredients for success in equestrian sports and navigating life's complexities. The challenges she faced and the setbacks she overcame strengthened her resolve and deepened her understanding of herself. She discovered her voice not as a rider but as a leader, mentor, artist, environmental advocate, and partner. She had learned that true strength lay not in flawlessness but in embracing imperfection, acknowledging vulnerability, and rising above adversity with courage and grace.

The future stretched before her, a vast and exciting canvas awaiting her next stroke. She had ambitious plans for her mentoring program, aiming to expand its reach and impact even further. Her research into equine biomechanics continued to progress, promising breakthroughs in equine healthcare and welfare. She and Sarah had plans for a large-scale public art installation that would resonate deeply with audiences and provoke meaningful dialogue about the importance of ethical treatment of animals and environmental responsibility. Competitions, arena excitement, pushing limits—all exhilarating. These ceased being ultimate goals.

The quiet contentment she felt wasn't the complacency of someone who had reached the peak of their aspirations; it was the tranquil confidence of a woman who had found her true north, her compass pointing towards a future prosperous in purpose, passion, and unwavering dedication. Her journey continued. And with Apollo, her steadfast companion, by her side, she was ready to embrace whatever challenges or triumphs the future might bring. Her life, a testament to the transformative power of perseverance, self-belief, and unwavering dedication to one's passions, unfolded a breathtaking panorama of endless possibilities before her. The path ahead was clear, and she was ready to ride.

Chapter 55: A Message of Hope

The moon, a silver disc in the inky sky, cast a soft glow on the rolling Kentucky hills. Jammie sat on her porch swing, a mug of warm chamomile tea warming her hands. Apollo, her magnificent Friesian stallion, stood patiently in the paddock nearby, his dark coat shimmering under the moonlight. He seemed to sense her quiet contemplation, his large, intelligent eyes following her every move. The years passed, a blur of competitions, triumphs, setbacks, and profound personal growth. She vividly recalled the Grand Prix, the product of years' dedication, yet it no longer defined her. It marked a pivotal point, propelling her self-discovery journey, culminating in profound peace and contentment.

Quiet confidence had replaced the insecurity that had once plagued her, the crippling self-doubt that had threatened to derail her dreams — a deep-seated belief in her abilities. She had learned that failure wasn't the opposite of success; it was an integral part of the process, a valuable teacher that had honed her resilience and strengthened her resolve. Difficulties and self-doubt shaped her into who she is today. She now embraces challenges, learns from failures, and refuses to let flaws define her.

Her relationship with Apollo had evolved beyond a mere rider-horse partnership. It was a deep connection — a silent understanding forged through years of shared experiences, mutual trust, and unwavering support. He was her confidante, her partner, her friend. Their communication went beyond words, a subtle exchange of cues, a shared understanding that transcended language barriers. She had learned to listen to him, read his subtle body language, and understand his needs and limits. This intuitive connection extended far beyond the world of competitive dressage. This bond enriched her life in countless ways, providing unwavering support and unconditional love.

Having found her passion for helping inexperienced riders, she dedicated herself to sharing her skills and knowledge. A desire to share her love of the sport and train the next generation of equestrians. She uniquely blended mindfulness practices and technical training in her program. Under her expert guidance, her students not only significantly improved their equestrian skills but also experienced a notable increase in emotional resilience, mental fortitude, and self-awareness, transforming their overall well-being. Recognizing their shared potential and passion, she inspired them, just as others had inspired her. Witnessing their progress filled her with a deeper sense of purpose than any personal achievement ever could.

Her research into equine biomechanics continued to flourish, yielding exciting discoveries and innovations in equine healthcare and welfare. Her work had a far-reaching impact, improving the lives of horses and contributing to a greater understanding of their physiology and athletic potential. She dedicated her expertise to promoting equine well-being, ensuring horse safety and comfort, advocating for ethical treatment, and contributing to sustainable equestrian practices. She didn't limit her dedication to horse welfare to her stable;

The art she created with Sarah continued to resonate with audiences, sparking conversations about the ethical treatment of animals, environmental sustainability, and the power of art to effect social change. Their exhibitions drew large crowds, and their powerful imagery inspired people to take action and make a difference. They were using their art to raise awareness, to advocate for change, and to promote a more ethical and responsible approach to the world around them. Although the recognition they received was gratifying, it was their deeper purpose and positive impact that fueled their passion.

John had been by her side throughout this journey. Their life together was a testament to their shared values, mutual respect, and unwavering commitment to each other. They were a strong, unified couple, and their shared values strengthened their connection. They had built a life rich in purpose that reflected their shared values and dedication to creating a better world.

Jammie reflected on her journey, feeling profoundly grateful. The journey had been challenging, fraught with moments of doubt and uncertainty. However, it was also gratifying, filled with triumphs, deep connections, and the profound satisfaction of knowing she had used her talents to make a meaningful difference in the world. Self-doubt once consumed her; now, she's a confident, compassionate, driven woman. She learned genuine success stems from internal fulfillment, not external rewards.

The future stretched before her, brimming with possibilities. She had ambitious plans for her mentoring program, research, and art. She looked forward to future competitions, not as a pursuit of validation but as opportunities to test her skills, push her limits, and share her love of dressage with the world. But underlying all her aspirations was a deep sense of peace, a quiet contentment born of self-acceptance, resilience, and a profound understanding of her potential.

Jammie realized that her journey, despite its hardships, was far from over. Unmapped territory stretched ahead, filled with both challenges and adventure, yet she welcomed it. With Apollo at her side, she felt there was nothing she couldn't face.

Acknowledgments

Above all, I am incredibly thankful to all the individuals who have a passion for horses, as they served as the inspiration for this story. I am consistently filled with a sense of wonder and admiration because of your clear passion and unwavering dedication to these incredible animals. The Youth Dressage Horse members deserve special recognition, a talented group of young artists, for their vibrant paintings that brought Apollo and Jammie's story to life, making their work truly stand out. Her creative vision gave the narrative a unique and captivating form, which enhanced the story.

This book would not have been possible without the unwavering support and encouragement of my family, to whom I am eternally grateful. I am grateful for your support of my goals and for being part of this experience. I will forever be grateful for your presence, because your love and faith have consistently been my guiding light. You have provided me with steadfast support, always encouraged me, and served as a true inspiration in my life. You and I share ownership of this book equally.

I am also extremely grateful to my illustrator, Karen Shayler, and my editor, Roxana Coumans, for their essential assistance and encouragement throughout the process of publishing this book. The tale that has come to life would not exist in its current form if it were not for your observant eye, your insightful feedback , and the incredible amount of patience you have shown. Because of your commitment to excellence and confidence in its success, this project has truly flourished.

In addition, I would like to express my gratitude for the invaluable guidance and expertise offered by the people who reviewed my work, among them my mother, Billie Aylesworth, who is associated with Diamond B Dressage Horses. We believe that your insights and feedback have truly enhanced the story, lending it both authenticity and depth. Your passion for horses and dedication to achieving the highest standards consistently serve as a source of inspiration for me.

To all the readers who have joined Jammie and Apollo on this adventure, we extend our gratitude for your encouragement and excitement. The existence of this book is because of your fondness for stories, along with your faith in the enchantment of friendship and the act of never giving up. We sincerely hope that this narrative will serve as a source of motivation, prompting you to pursue your ambitions, cultivate your friendships, and treasure the relationships that add value to your existence.

About the Author

Brett Shayler, an author, has been passionate about horses and the natural world his entire life. Raised on a ranch surrounded by diverse animals, his storytelling vividly reflects the profound and enduring connections between people and the animals they cherish and care for throughout their lives. Drawing inspiration from his family's vast acreage and the wild horses that roam freely upon it, Brett lovingly crafts heartwarming tales that not only celebrate the bonds of friendship but also extol the virtues of a deep respect for the natural world and the remarkable connections that exist in the relationships between people and animals. Through his books, he hopes to cultivate curiosity, compassion, and a thirst for knowledge in young readers. Brett often escapes to nature, hiking and observing wildlife, finding inspiration for his writing away from his desk. Brett proudly holds membership in both the prestigious National Dressage Horse Association and the equally esteemed American Quarter Horse Association, demonstrating his deep commitment to these organizations and the equestrian world.